A New Way to Stop Breathing

Dillon Droege

Copyright © Dillon Droege 2015

All rights reserved.

ISBN: 1518670474

ISBN-13: 978-1518670473

FOR
MOM & DAD

4

TABLE OF CONTENTS

ELDER MONSTERS	**7**
RUSSIAN MYSTICISM	**30**
THE DARK HEAT	**46**
DOWN THE OLD BEND	**53**
THURSDAY	**74**
HOW TO FEEL BETTER	**95**

6

ELDER MONSTERS.

I.

Emmett is awake early enough to hear the newspaper trucks come lumbering off the freeway, all parts of their exoskeleton shaking off foreign ice and snow. He can hear them shivering across Queens Boulevard, clattering hard over the exchange.

It's early.

Quiet black.

Nightmares these days have been warding off all serious forms of sleep. And so Emmett is awake, shaking off nightmares like they were foreign ice. Until spines of light find the translucent parts in the eastern wall of his apartment and lance in, causing his nightmares, photophobic, to track back to the more disreputable sectors of his cerebral cortex. Its unlighted tombs and its cinereous thieves' rows.

Then he's vertical.

He's dressed.

He always checks the stove before he leaves. The sky outside, the way it's easing from dark of night to daybreak, has the look of a dying shiner, healing its way from purple to yellow. Whatever morning cloudscape there is degenerates behind the cemetery, broken down for scraps and fed into the mouth of fire: a white-hot sun that sits directly behind the nominal backlit Calvary, throwing a crucifixion shadow forward.

Mornings he can hear church bells. Out the door. Down an elevator. Overnight, frost had climbed the steps to his apartment and so Emmett takes the grade leading away from his building with caution, then turns, and he hears the church bells first, sounding off hollow and gigantic, before the great yellow architecture of the church comes pulling into frame.

Pigeons break off the Saint Theresa. Their loose geometry dips below the seven line. The tracks reverberate in protest to the speed and weight of a train, and the buzz-through is experienced almost triply by those in the station's umbra: seen, felt, and heard; a shiver in the elevated rails and its reinforcing elements, a vibratory sensation in all neighboring shoe-soles. This, the church bells, and the street noise, plus a jetliner laying sonic tracks across the airspace overhead, make for a world of noise.

It's one part elegiac, three parts cacophonous.

Today, served over ice.

Emmett makes a habit of arriving early, wherever it is he's arriving at. And so he's developed also a keen nose for finding decent coffee, to support the corollary habit of killing time in someplace proximal to the rendezvous. This morning, he ducks into a market; one of those old Asian markets with slat plastic front doors where the labyrinthine aisles snake you skintight through all sorts of Far World grotesqueries: five alarm vegetables with slick polygons of greased pork, nontensile noodles in nuoc mam, cold squid, unboxed cat food.

Back outside he places his coffee on the level surface inside a phone booth where once a phone book must've sat. Morning in full swing, with all its accessory traffic: vehicular, pedestrian, otherwise. A man wearing one mitten is unloading newspapers from a truck and re-stacking the bales of them onto the sidewalk and the plastic on these newspaper bunches is harder than all other plastic and so the man uses his non-gloved hand to open a box-cutter with which he makes diagonal cuts across the plastic, unbridling the taut stacks and allowing them to exhale. Another man takes the papers inside. Spirits lift out of Emmett's coffee as it seeks heat-equilibrium. Acknowledging the comparative heat of the coffee gives Emmett a reflexive chill, so he cinches the belt of his black trench coat. Too old now to harbor much in the way of personal vainglory, he rebuffs that inner impulse.

At first.

Because maybe there's some vanity still extant, and that part fashions himself a master of the crepuscular, his cloak pantherine, his eyes gleeding in the cold wash of morning...

The payphone rings, the anachronistic conversational standby of cut-rate criminals and knee-breaking creeps and cornermen and ne'er-do-wells everywhere; Emmett doesn't like them. The sound of the payphone breaks away from its physical frame, a still and rigidly metallic thing, whose stillness and strict metalwork belie its clarion racket.

He answers the phone, listens to it.

They're telling him the make, the model of the car.

He waits over a cigarette. A Viceroy, from a soft pack. A small comfort, as familiar to him as the isobars of wrinkles in his face, or the architecture of the old hands he watches as they work his lighter. Talismanic, warming, and transportable, are the cigarettes and their compatriot lighter, extracted from and then tucked back into the depths of the black trench.

Cars, trucks and taxis working up Queens Boulevard in déjà vu fractals. That could be the car. That could be the car, he thinks. Until the coffee is done. The cigarette too. That could be the car.

It isn't though.

It's repeatedly not the car.

The tap has been cracked and now the sun is bleeding light like a sieve. It's an omnidirectional white light, that carries with it heat. In the scattered shadows it is still more arctic morning. Even the traceries under fire escapes and sterile trees drape a net of cold on passers-by. But in that unbroken, cold-filtered sunlight there is a resilient little warmth, and so Emmett tosses his empty coffee cup into a corner pail and he stands in a big brilliant patch of the stuff, beyond the shadows of the cinema bulbs and the elevated train station, where the sun comes cascading in over the suprastructure.

In it, inside this merciful spotlight of Januarian apricity, he feels good. He can feel the good in things. He is somehow reaffirmed of the good things and their sometimes precarious existence in this mostly wretched part of the world.

But lo, the dualistic nature of the human psyche. Once, he'd had love in his heart. And the love was big and the love was pure. It was the world that was wrong. What he knew now was that even if you were careful, the world would try to hurt you. And repeatedly, testing your thresholds. Sure, doing good felt good. Being bad though, Emmett had learned, was more profitable. It was the cannier retaliation, when the world seemed out for blood.

Over time, this line of thinking stripped away the good in him. Erosion is a slow but persistent force. So it was only eventually, that the good side of him was ripped flat, like an upturned penny's face in the rain.

The car finally pulls up and it's a cantankerous old Crown Victoria in a color called Norsea Blue. Emmett knows this, the name *Norsea Blue*, and from far off the look of a Crown Victoria, having spent a lot of the late eighties and early nineties traveling around in lots of Crown Victorias with lots of Crown Victoria enthusiasts prideful about their means of conveyance and strangely vocal about their vehicles' paintjobs, which seemed to inordinately favor the color Norsea Blue. Maybe because of New York's skew towards the Democratic Party in the late '80s. And here Emmett is once again, human incarnate of history's tendency to repeat itself, working the trick handle on a back door of a blue Crown Vic.

He gets in slowly. The vehicle reincorporates into traffic. The city moves at a different speed from the inside of a moving car. Everyone's life is shorter; their stories much more brief. The bridge sprouts up from the Earth. Life coming up big behind the Silvercup sign.

Big, chrome-plated Manhattan, wearing the morning sun high across its eastern flank, is ready for business.

Here we go.

She lights incense and comes back to bed, followed by the smoke, which starts thin from the point of the stick and then drifts flatter and more broadly out, following the contours of an invisible land. She bites his ear. That's the first point of contact, two rows of teeth clamped delicately around an ear. Then, layers of clothes rubbed off by friction: the friction between their two bodies and the friction between her body and his rough hands, and then friction between them and the environment, the bed, the sheets; like how a snake sloughs off skin. There's more to her than he remembers, but there is something satisfying to the bulk, an implication of lastingness. Her tongue taking familiar alpine routes down his torso. She's taken these roads so long she leaves the map at home. Her red curtains lit from behind remind him of when he used to hold a flashlight under his palm as a child, the semitransparency of rubricated flesh, the darker vertical fibers and runs in the material are the curtain's veins.

He has had this thought before.

He has been in this room before.

She's ebbing and elongating, a retraction/eduction process he's so familiar with he could use it as a crude metronome. And would, too. These little timings, her subroutines- he feels about them like a pianist might his device. There is a trust and gratitude too simple to necessitate being spoken of aloud.

The room fills with her breath, his breath, the thin sound of a cat scraping on the outside of the bedroom door, the smell of her Guerlinade, the dense and ancient smell of the mattress and, moreover, the smell of incense smoke, which exists on two planes: is fragrant and visible both, as it flattens into dales and goes rolling up over false snowpeaks. She gathers force, a ritual of sexual crescendo that begins when she anticipates orgasm, as the smoke is drawing new maps, engineering a gossamer highlands' rolling fog, existing temporarily above the bed.

This whole affair began as a badger game. Believe it or not. Back when they were both bad people, they'd pulled into each other's orbits per the cohesive nature of villains. Emmett was married at the time, spending too much time out of the house under the fragile auspices of "working late." Eventually the ice of that logic broke and he fell irretrievably in. *She* was arm candy back then. An argument made for the barbed lure as the seventh simple machine- glimmering in shoulder pads and kitten heels and peplum. The angler on the end, her shank-wrought beau, was something of a criminal polymath. If there was ever any chatter about a crooked way to bleed someone of a buck, you could believe that he was listening. Low-yield loan shark, part-time welfare defrauder, dishonest mechanic. With some sort of blackmail in mind, she'd seduced Emmett. But Emmett was divorced now and the Mechanic had his reckoning a decade ago but even with the illicit framework having fallen away, whatever chemistry it was that'd magnetized them in the first place it, well, it just still worked.

    The particular terms of the arrangement met and completed, Emmett was once again vertical, dressed, picking his cigarettes up off the fruitwood credenza.

    It is a human impulse to assign meaning to relationships, sexual or otherwise. Though the intimate ones did seem to beckon harder, Emmett knew. And he'd be lying if he were to say that he didn't find himself, at times, contemplating the deeper beauty. Even now, as he watches her move about the room, his daydreams need manufacturing. A purpose beyond simple contact must be found, is what he thinks, as she quietly repairs herself with clothes, perfume.

    Orgasm for him was only a brief respite. During the whitewash of carnal unwinding, it was temporarily easy for Emmett to stop thinking. And it was an easy stigma to get yourself associated with, becoming the guy that only lived to work out a fuck. But while Emmett didn't feel like a slave to his libido, it was impossible for him to deny how much easier things were for him post hoc. It was easy for him, to let float free the pins of memory, in the afterglow pursuant to intercourse. As his reflex to dwell felt bushed, over-thirsty, and diminished. One faculty ceding to another, like biting your tongue to quell a headache.

But every second removed from that blinding climax made it harder for him to forget. Forget the innumerable precursory choices that he'd incontrovertibly made throughout the years, some good but mostly bad, that'd led him to this half-dark room. Some of the choices were hard to make. Some came so easy they didn't seem much like choices at all.

The lady, lost in a post-coital dreamworld all her own, applies moisturizer in an unreeling pattern of limbs that is codified somewhere in Emmett's long memory; legs plumb to the ground, arms akimbo, hands sailing themselves around herself.

Sex here, well, it was beginning to feel like something he'd call second nature. And that- that was a dangerous categorization. Because even if the act itself, the sex, was pure *now*, it had been evil that'd led them there, bought the deed. It was immorality that'd laid down carpet and it was Emmett himself, by his lonesome, that'd set up romantic shop. That so much was true. Orgasm was a reliable good feeling. And there was an inertia in good feelings- a happy indolent lamprey adjoined happily to personal happiness' underbelly, teeth sunk, happy to stay. Hard to unsuckle willingly from the blood flow born of happiness, Emmett knew. But this whole little ecosystem reeked of complacency.

Oh, and Emmett was old enough to know that built right into every sense of complacency was a foundation of fear. And he knew fear's cement stayed wet, ready to trap uncertain feet, when they didn't move quick enough across its surface. No one of these circumstances operates alone. Emmett could feel the reality of the situation in a piecemeal way, felt the bricolage of tenure buttressing his situation, the screws and struts and cantilevers and bulkheads, pressed indelicately against his skin, holding him here.

They had all required nails to install.

And then, as always, Emmett's almost Calvinist submission to the transpirations at hand. It's that perfect scene, where the tea kettle begins creating steam, and the plant in her kitchen window bends affectionately at the glass the same way her cats use their cheeks when they're plying for love, and he sets down cross-legged at the low, square kitchen table, and white heat comes in and fills the room that they co-occupy, him and her, garden sun illuminating this old familiar, a diorama of two aging stars, emitting softly their failing lights, strangers only to themselves.

It was a brown and white bus stop town, where the summers were long, and when winter did come, the snow seemed to fall already dirty.

The old part of this old town used to *course*-- with an almost palpable energy. And this energy-schema? All permanent residents seemed to be hooked up to it. Some of the shadier itinerants too. And this very old part of town, well, its lifeblood was cocaine. The assumption and redistribution of which kept all the moving parts moving. (And *how*). Nearly all of the townsfolk played a role. Because it takes a village, as they say. Some played roles simply with their silence. Roles of inaction, roles of feigned ignorance in the presence of investigatory or judicial forces, etc. But most played more corporal roles. One of Emmett's old associates called it an illicit circulatory system. Phrased it as such: the dealers and users were the arteries and veins, carrying product or cash to or away from the heart. Cops were the kidneys, trying to clean the blood. The street-level guys were the capillaries. The Boss, naturally, was the heart.

This particular associate was a ceaselessly irate *Napolitano* who, clad normally in his trademark lapped planes of denim, was always trying to indict a tyrant or unmask a conspiracy, as if life were an elaborate annoyance engineered by a trickster God; a problem that could somehow be talked out of, if talked at long and forcefully enough.

He and this associate used to light fireplace matches off their boot heels, to impress vicinal girls, Emmett remembers, whenever they were around some in public, leaning on their cars, or against storefront windows.

Should be noted: this associate's shoulder was all chip, and Emmett used to worry that if he ever ran out of things to rail against, he'd shut down. Like a loyal dog or dutiful machine. He'd find somewhere secluded to die having served his appointed task. See, he ran on the hate, lived for it even; he smoked a lot, and exhaled through his nose, and had two Yorkshire terriers, and a Hapsburg lip that made him talk funny. Eventually, he did find his way out from underneath the conspiracy. In 1993, this associate was killed for reasons that were never made perfectly clear though were, perhaps, obvious. He was beaten then strangled in a supermarket parking lot.

Some long and forgotten summer before that though, that one that was warmer in peoples' collective memories, they'd shared a place together, Emmet and this associate of his. It was a retrofit ADU, many-windowed and filled with furniture bought pennywise from the goodwill. Timeworn furniture, which'd been hauled laboriously up the back stairway, to the open space above an old garage. The garage itself was set back into the treeless property, and only ever used for storage, not for cars. The apartment and garage below, en masse, became something of an institution relative to the single-storied flatness of the surrounding neighborhood; an architectural gnomon that bent its shadow over adjacent pools, barbecues.

The apartment bloomed in summer, parachuted itself open in the seawind, and glutted itself on midsummer light, its big sky-blue window shutters clapping satisfyingly open, when they were opened, in the direction of distant Hewlett Bay.

Emmett's room was perfunctory, lacking affectation, intermediately tidy. Some books. His bedroom window faced south.

Shapeshifting women would pass through this room, and leave when they were done, and Emmett would smoke Viceroys out of his window feeling the velveteen heat of a putrid city, to which the sex sweat on his skin would entropically return, as he tapped ash into the black ashtray that he kept out on the balconette.

There was a bar they always went to.

In towns like this, there was always a bar that everyone always went to.

From the street, it didn't look like too much.

Just a red-colored bar door set flush into the bar brick, and so the only way you knew it was a bar at all was the worn set of dryland bollards that lined the front, just that scant decoration, open volcanic, resembling, sort of, the cigarettes people'd deposit into them before heading inside. Which they'd customarily do, drop their dead butt into the fissured-open top of a cracked bollard before pressing through that door, the one the color of half-boiled lobster. Then they're taking the long, slow curve of the gunwale shaped-bar towards the back. And, if it was daytime, they'd excuse the behind-the-scenes look of the place. The stalagmites of unpacked beer and stacks of inverted stools. The bar lights and overhead pool lights, which would be off but glowing some in the seep-in daylight. These dead lenses, when intermixed with some of the more regular incandescent daytime bulbglow, blanched all the bar fixtures, and gave the bar-set on the whole a roughhewn and premature look.

And in that uncooked light sat the Methuselahean full-timers: unshorn, uplit, into their cups, sucking at their daytime whiskeys.

But it wasn't all fun and Jameson.

The bar was a peripheral place of business. Under the guise of recreation, it was here the townspeople furtively conducted their dark commerce. It was in that tacitly accepted form the bar functioned as war room, agora, and unofficial wellhead of dim enterprise- a place enjoyed but sort of feared, in tense inequity, by all.

The utility of the place really being, of course, that pertinent business information could be clandestinely discussed there, provided adequate coverage, as it was, by the bar's natural capability to drown out sound; to aurally mask. Many a sotte voce bit of shoptalk was afforded safe passage, crook-to-crook, in this bar, at night. Wetskin summer nights where toughs extinguished cigarettes into each other's flesh to show (generally) unimpressed female onlookers that they could take a little pain. Emmett, and his contingent, well, their chosen line of work didn't have too early an opening bell, and so they borrowed heavily from groggy morning's physical efficiency and invested it backwards deep into long and drunken nights. Nights when the general tessitura of the bar ran its hot fever, when the tempo of beers being cheersed and consumed hit their nightly hypervelocity, when the high snap of billiard pyramids cracking apart multiplied with some of the more person-to-environment noises. When the mechanical interplay of drunken cockalorum men knocking drunkenly around their surroundings or howling loudly at the women caught in their blurry crosshairs got loud. Those misty, languorous women in high shorts and bad lipstick, who smacked their lips when they talked. When all of this, this standard conglomerate of bar-noise, plus the gangster bluster, plus the dark ancillary buzz, etc. made for a sort of three-sheeted tintinnabulation. It overrode the twenty-thousand-league subtext. And so anything whispered, anything spoken softly enough that its decibel level registered under the general din, was subdued, was said and heard and then died a death.

Sub vino, sub rosa, as they say.

The bar then a living, breathing cryptogram: cords of men in leather bombers, swigging Carta Blanca on trips between the jukebox and the pool table, or sequences of them knotted towards the back, where the two large fans pointed. Or plugged into stools in vaguely discernible patterns. Encompassing a mute network. Stifling a shared secret. A human mosaic of hush-hush, under-the-table, on the down, down low.

Outside the bar, there was the payphone. There was always also a payphone. Nights, they'd all take turns making phone calls on this one pay phone, out back, under where the bar neon painted a diffuse double of itself on the clabbered moonscape of bar-wall, light soft on the thick buttermilk-yellow paintjob and into its many pocks, wherever all the local luminaries who deigned themselves worthy tattooed their so-thought indelible sobriquet, and where commoners only extinguished their cigarettes. And because this particular swathe of brickface was scrubbed at only biannually, or so, the wall became a palimpsest of local drunkards past, its current stratum serving as reading fodder for those on-hold or between calls.

Who were *they*? Well, Emmett, and his former roommate, of course. The owner of the bar was old and fat and was non-participatory by the time Emmett had entered the professional fray, though some minor legend of his former prowess still circulated. Something about taking an eyeball out with a wine opener. But who knows if stories like that are ever true. His nephew though, the bar owner's, was still involved in a semi-serious way, and he ran with a small circle of truck robbers that of course used the bar as a cash laundromat. Then there was the stable of trusted hitters. And a few younger kids who lived over by Beth David. A few part-timers. A big Greek ex-con with a dead eye named Anatolios. And some of Nini Bruschi's boys out of Passaic.

Always with the eyes. A real Oedipal chord lurking somewhere under the criminal waterline, begging to be plucked. Or worse.

Regardless the level of violence intrinsic to their particular subclass of work, everyone, and Emmett means everyone, had their own sidearm. Which they compared, like business cards. Berettas, or maybe a Taurus later on, and H&K's, and blued .357s and Glocks with 9mm Parabellum. Or SIGs made with replicate Cold War-era plates in Laotian or Burmese machine shops and transported over brown water in the underbellies of old junks and sold in places like East New York and Flint Township and Lemon City. Normally to semiprofessional scumbags- and cheap ones.

Of course, conscience is a comparative game, and so long as no one had much of it, they could all cooperatively daisy-chain, in blithe forced-ignorance, across the chasm of imminent guilt. So you'd be hard-pressed to find anyone who self-diagnosed as scumbag.

Emmett's time in what by only loose conscription would be considered "the business" was profitable, perilous, and filthy with guys just like him. Guys who chose to eschew the title of scumbag; who were variations on a broader theme: caricatures of cinematic ruffians, slim men who languished in the green light of billiard halls, beer-drunk and pugilistic and lightly-armed, pool cues and pool bridges slung flat across backs clad in white t-shirts and beer mugs gripped tight in gearbox fists, like so many Paul Newmans, and men who called themselves knock-off artists, as if you didn't already know who the buncos were, because the buncos moved in flagrant cabals, bound by the cartoon of their own collective Pall Mall smoke, with their conspiratorial tails trailing behind them almost visibly, communicating the scheme and whisper between them so perceptibly that you could identify it on each of them individually, like how you could spot the guys who'd recently gotten laid because they smelled of old perfume, these the same guys who ran loose game against other knockaround guys, the guys who modified their weapons with potatoes and old handsaws and rimfire, and felt glad at least that they weren't the men who had punted themselves deep into financial holes and then paid rent for the plot else ate dirt, who, these creatures of the grave we're talking now, the everlastingly in debt, well these poor sons of bitches had two shadows, their own and then the graybeard men who visited them daily and carried handwritten rolodices in the breast pockets of their 3-piece suits, because they had been in the business for a long, long time, and so used payphones exclusively, just like they learned in movies, but who employed younger men to do the wetwork, younger men who carried their Mossbergs in gym bags or on their shoulders like Louisville Sluggers, and spent most of their time brandishing claw hammers at welshers and ideological dissenters, considering this their *joie de vivre* even, and then so the lot of them, the warthog enforcers, the junkies, the various units of relay, the captains, the splinter factions and the sectarians working the racketeer 1099, the network in toto, they occupied, like little illicit electrons in quantum criminal flux, the covalence around a nucleus, which was the racetrack, to and from which they figuratively ran the numbers, when they weren't carrying cans of beer into and out of the OTBs, or driving their Iroc-Zs and Mustangs and black Firebirds with red skunkstripes, and Chargers and Plymouth Road Runners, and they pulsed with the amphetamine rhythm of the town, and were always either reporting back or waiting on calls, these human conduits between rolodex and payphone, crude facsimiles of a specific type of criminal alluded to in media and stored somewhere in the communal public consciousness, playing basketball halfheartedly with unlit cigarettes inserted behind their ears, fucking girls with Irish names in the basements of their parents' homes, calling local cops by their badge names, staying up late, taking too much liquor, scratching deep at the well of all the old clichés.

Though, of course, they didn't realize this at the time.

And, actually, don't hold Emmett to the perfect truthfulness of any of this. All of these memories, in retrospect, seem sepia-toned and a little scorched around the edges due in part to a love affair he'd had at the time, with Seagram's Seven Crown, which had reached its most torrid, low-O_2 peaks during the three years or so that he'd lived over that garage.

Anyway, that's what life was like, for him, back then.

IV.

Some meditations.

i. Every generation thinks they own the present. That the modern day is theirs. Time only helps to skew the angle. Here's how it really is: the young think everything is up for grabs, the men think they're grabbing the bull by the horns, but only the old, and only if they're lucky, have the bull's head stuffed and mounted on their wall. And these lucky old, only they can waltz into their living room, to hear something sweet and lentissimo come unspooling from their old record player. Only they can set a small glass of their preferred brown poison down on the small table they bought to sit next to their old chesterfield. Only they can sit on it, an old trusted couch, when they wish to remember their kill, or, more generally, when they want to think about how invigorating it must've been to feel that need to kill. And maybe then, in all their elder shrewdness, maybe only they can also lament that what they should've known all along is how insignificant the kill was in retrospect, how small a piece of the universe was ever really available to them at all.

ii.   Remorse is an aggregate poison, like mercury. And it'll stick to the walls of your soul, the ectoplasm that leaches from a guilty conscience. Unless you can somehow scrub yourself clean, from time to time; unless you've got the mental detergent necessary. Some men have it. Some don't.

iii. A lot of people like to speculate about what Hitler was like as a child. Because it's not immediately graspable, to the regular human, how baby Hitler, in his booties and white frock and frilled collar, all doe-eyed and fat-cheeked, grew up to be a monster. It's hard, back-extrapolating the interstitial steps between. Just like it's hard to imagine how protozoa evolved into humans. But we came up with charts for that. It is not hard for [me] to imagine. All that's necessary is imagining each of the individual juncture points where a human psyche might be negatively affected by outside stimuli. And then it's not about imagining anything too grievous, in the way trauma sometimes leads to a complete emotional overhaul, which- that's the sole domain of comic book characters. It's about imagining, instead, the recurrent modica of evil that might take hold in lieu of orts of goodness, and then tracing the cumulative effect.

    a. And then accepting the possibility of a saturation point from whence there's no return. Accepting that enough inflowing evil sees the subject cross some sort of threshold, and then accepting that from there there'd be no escape. That there exists an evil deep enough that descent into it makes the subject irredeemably bad. (e.g. Hitler, whom, even with the right PR team, probably couldn't have scrubbed clean the image he'd earned for himself over the course of the great war. Had he not shot himself in that bunker, of course, cutting any and all speculation short.) And that, conversely, even after fifty wrong turns a series of right turns could waylay the descent into full evil, theoretically, if this threshold hasn't yet been crossed. How the descent into evil could be tempered with an equal amount of good. The way a line comprised of many small deviations, left and right, might look straight from far enough away.

    b. And then accepting of course, that the absorption of outside evil, or the harboring of evil thoughts, *eo ipso*, does not make a person evil but rather acting upon these impulses, behaving evilly, is what counts, obviously.

    c. And then taking into account an individual's personalized management of evil. The likelihood of one's manufacturing an evil out of a borderline innocuous incident or, alternatively, maybe one's sharp eye for silver linings, and the subsequent neutralization of incoming evil. And then adjusting for these tendencies.

d. And ignoring an evil person's capacity for also good. Ignoring, on karmic terms, the possibility of net goodness despite gross badness on the part of the evildoer in question.

e. And, naturally, ignoring the subjective nature of evil and the potential faultiness of human comprehension of both evil but also, really, goodness. And so trying to forge onwards despite the fact that evaluating the yin-yang of evil-good makes qualifying and then quantifying "evil" a logistical nightmare, and makes the whole pursuit seem impossible or even frivolous, all things considered, given just this creaky interpretation-apparatus. And so then, having to adopt a sort of homogenized, averaged worldview of evil and good, added up and then divided across a representative sample of opinion. And going from there.

The phone is ringing. A landline, another antique.

-Hello, and pleasantries. And then,

-A briefing: quick rundown of the past however many months, salient points served and returned, various daily groundstrokes sparking new tangential conversational filaments, pinging off the common theme. And then,

-A spelunk into deeper discussion:

E: "I believe, that it's human nature to try goodness. It's only afterwards that we resort to evil. Having seen, sometimes time and time again, the fruitlessness."

"Of being good?"

E: "Of being good."

"Seems these days, kids are quicker on the draw. Readier."

E: "Maybe the stakes are higher."

"Maybe."

E: "Remember us though. It didn't take much goading for us."

"It's true."

E: "Do you remember that winter? That we drove down to the shore? To Wildwood? Because my cousin knew a guy with pot that we could sell? What were we, fifteen years old? And we met him on the boardwalk? And the whole ride back we thought that we were gangsters?"

"That was a long, long time ago."

E: "That was it."

"That was what?"

E: "I mean, that's what started it all. In a way."

"I guess, maybe."

E: "Sometimes, I look back. And feel like since then, I haven't had a moment's rest. Like I've been looking back over my shoulder for forty years."

"There were good times."

E: "There were. I'm not saying there were no good times. But always, a tension."

"Well, that was the cost. Always a cost."

E: "Was it too high a cost?"

"It's hard for me to say."

E: "It is. It's impossible, looking back. Wondering if it was worth it."

"It's an ordinary thing, I think, to wonder."

E: "To wonder in general, or to wonder if it was all worth it?"

"Right. To wonder if it was all worth it. We can't be the only old men with regrets."

E: "Regret. You know what's interesting? There's no real opposite of regret, is there? Contentment? There's only passive agency in contentment. You don't feel content as incisively as you feel the sting of regret. And how do you ever know when it's over? How do you know the good times are over, so you can commence looking back upon them fondly?"

"When it's over? Is it ever over?"

E: "Exactly my point. There's little to no wait time with regret. Regret'll find you quick."

"I think, you're right. About how it's impossible to ever really exhale, maybe. But, finding little pieces of calm. I try to. And that's not impossible. Finding momentary grace."

E: "I don't want moments. I don't want to live moment to moment. I want something final. I want peace."

"And what's peace?"

E: "Peace is an old inn with open rooms at the end of a long road."

"And once you're in there?"

E: "No more walking."

RUSSIAN MYSTICISM.

I can remember the first time I realized I wasn't afraid to die.

I remember it was summer, and I was only fifteen. Before I learned to drive. Before I knew that only twelve percent of air flight fatalities occur during cruising altitude.

In my seat, I remember looking out the porthole window, at an abstract painting the color of wheat and rivers.

I remember jockeying for position and stability -turbulence- arms akimbo in the coffin-shaped bathroom of a DC-10 on this predawn flight to Oklahoma City.

When you meet your pilot, if he looks tired, or his eyes are half-glazed over and his breath smells like martini olives, or he's wearing a Calvin and Hobbes tie—I wouldn't worry too much.

Most crashes are caused by mechanical errors or bad weather.

I remember the plane started rocking violently, and as I braced myself, wedging my shoulder into the wall mirror and stiff-arming the miniature sink, I found out that there's an oxygen mask that pops out of the ceiling in the bathroom there too. I remember I just put it on and finished up smiling.

I heard a story about a man named Sergei. At fourteen, Sergei tested a homemade pistol and it backfired in his hands, sending a bullet through his left eye and out through the side of his head, blinding him forever.

After that Sergei could feel color with his fingertips. He could diagnose a headache by standing near a person, palms upturned, his unseeing white eyes wandering around the sky, his open mouth breathing in aura.

"Good aura is of light shades, yellow or orange. And the bad aura is colored black or brown," he said once.

Sergei literally stared death in the face, then took a bullet in the skull that caused one blindness and cured another.

"Isn't that what you'd say, if you had to say something?" He'd ask, as he ran his soft fingertips around a fiery redhead's scalp saying,

"Red."

I heard this story from an overweight man while we were both waiting for a flight out of Hartsfield-Jackson, over coffee that had gone cold since I'd gotten it from my hotel's lobby. I was silent for a long time before I said, "Fifty-one percent of all plane accidents happen during the final approach or landing."

He just brushed milk froth out of his red moustache.

"I was in a plane accident once," I said.

I'm walking out of JFK, through automated doors, talking on my cell phone and wheeling luggage when a black car pulls up in front of me.

"I need to catch an eastbound train as soon as possible," I tell the driver, leaning into the passenger side window. "Just drive me to Jamaica."

He says, smiling, "We just go to Mineola, okay? Lots of trains, less traffic."

"I don't have a lot of money."

He says, "Just get in."

So I jump into the back of his black Lincoln, stash my suitcase lengthwise in the ample legroom, and marvel at the cold leather and the array of lukewarm beers.

"Feel free," he says.

So I open a bottle of beer.

He takes off at insane speeds, hitting the loops and clover bends that lead to the parkway with such intensity I wonder for a second if I might not take off again. Back to the skies. He cuts through lanes and cars yield to him like how a shark swims through schools of fish. When he banks hard across an intersection, gliding only feet in front of cutoff cars sliding on screeching brakes, he just smiles, and asks,

"What is it?" He turns to me, putting his hand on the passenger seat's headrest. He says,

"Everyone is in such terrible rush."

I take a sip of the beer.

His tires spring over a short median, sending the car reeling. Blowing a red light amid a chorus of car horns.

"What is it? I cannot smile?"

Out of habit I check his license, laminated and displayed in the pane of lucite that frames the back and front seat dividing wall: *Dmitry Garnaev*.

Passing a gas station, he laments, "Oh, look at this closed down. A friend of mine used to own. Waste of good location."

It's odd, I told him, "I used to pass this place when I was a kid."

He knows too much about gas station ownership. He knows that rising gas prices actually spell disaster for chain owners. He knows that in 1989 government legislation uprooted all of the steel tanks and forced in more environmentally friendly fiberglass composites. He knows that most tanks are about ten feet in diameter.

"You must've been pretty good friends with that guy, huh?"

"I can understand why he has to shut down," he says. "What the government does not take in taxes they collect with citations. Do you know how much ticket is for *ah-deen* leaky hose?"

He holds up one finger.

I didn't know.

"Ten thousands," he says, shaking his head.

"Hey, money isn't everything, right?" The anthem of the blue collar, I sigh, lifting up my beer and tilting it backwards in that time-honored way, taking a slow and conscientious swig.

His rejoinder is a rehearsed joke, an automatic response he has tailored to our moment, another chorus for the working class:

"People who fly first class die first!"

He laughs, but I say,

"Is that really such a terrible thing?"

"Rasputin, he lived in a cellar for years before being assumed to the royal court. Before he became the scourge of the Winter Palace."

At the time, I was leafing through a SkyMall catalogue.

I remember I was drinking a vodka and soda with an old looking freeze-dried lemon bobbing unenthusiastically on its surface.

"That's where he prayed, underground. The rough-mannered Khlyst. Son of a drunken cantor and survivor of two drowned siblings. There in the cellar, he prayed and repented."

I was hearing this from some scholar with a spade-tip goatee, bad breath, and a salt-and-pepper blazer with beige elbow pads. I remember the way he curled his fingers around wisps of his stringy hair as he spoke, orating from a phantom textbook.

"He was a horse whisperer you know."

The scholar nods solemnly.

"Imagine this," he says, through tobacco-rot teeth.

And I did.

One night, as a child, Rasputin fell ill. Running high temperatures, sweating hot bullets into the icy Russian winter.

He could hear his parents downstairs. To ward off the cold, the mother and the father and their friends were huddled in the evening room, drinking vodka in dark shawls, woolen dresses, hand-stitched cotton bonnets; the rings on their wrinkled fingers shine, almost in reverse, the glassy bezoars black as oil in the dappled lamplight. Over bread and milk, hard cheese and pickles, they smoked and discussed a local horse theft.

So, I imagined the boy. A boy: frail skinny with eyes that shone like subarctic water, pointing out the thief from the balustrade with one quavering arm.

Repeating: 'Thief!'

Knowing he was right.

Knowing because he had heard it too.

I thought of the mother with an almost impossibly big mole on her left cheek. I thought of her scuttling over, wrapping the boy's white body in her tasseled shawl, apologizing for her son's fever dreams. I thought of the dad, in gray clothes fastened with boiled brown leather, carrying the boy over his back to bed. I thought of the mother, making the sign of the cross.

So, imagine what the townspeople must've thought when the boy turned out to be right?

"You know, Rasputin was invited into a cellar for dinner, fed cyanide-laced wine and cake, shot, beaten and drowned," said the scholar.

Then he took a bite of a ham sandwich which he had taken out of his pocket.

"17A," I say. "That's the exit to my grandparents' house. What a coincidence."

The driver smiles warmly, takes his eyes off the road to turn up the air conditioner a little, and says, "Gasoline tanks, UTCs they are called, are buried bedded in pea gravel, five to six feet below the ground."

"Like graves."

"Under those circular crown-valves you drive over when you go to fill up."

His frenzied tachometer swings violently as he jams up and down on the gearshift.

I said,

"These statistics defy trends. Pilots and planes aren't getting any worse, but they're not getting any better. It's chaos theory."

"Gasoline can pollute the ground for years. Seep into your pipes. Poison your drinking water."

"They started keeping track around the turn of the century," I said. "In 1931 if you were on a plane that was involved in an accident where at least one person died, you had a twenty-one percent chance of living."

"Here I thought it was all dead, or all alive. Big boom."

"Well, yeah, that's what I used to think. Planes go down hard. That image of metal scraps floating around the ocean in a circle of shark fins gets burned into your mind. Thing is, nowadays, same situation, you've got a twenty-four percent chance of making it out alive."

"So, it gets a little better."

"Except it's gone up and down in every intervening decade for the last sixty years," I say, watching this town whir past at a hundred miles per hour.

"How did you say? Chaos."

I was searching for a number that could scare me again, but there was no pattern.

Everything came up short.

He said,

"In 1989 gas station owners are forced to switch over their tanks. The old steel ones corrode too easily; they leak into the earth. They make you switch to fiberglass reinforced plastic. Or composites. Steel covered in fiberglass gives interstitial space. They are called test wells, these small space between feeds to drainage pipes which can detect even slightest amount of leakage."

I thought of the interstitial space involved in midair, wingtip-to-wingtip crashes. Accidents where you don't die right off. Engine burnouts. Dark turbulence. I thought of the sky, thirty-thousand feet of interstitial space before the ground. I thought of falling bodies. Silhouettes like big, black rain.

"Remediation," he said, "is men coming in wearing white suits and they check the level and, how do you say, migration of water and soil contamination. Then they tell you how long before you grow tomatoes."

Just two men with minds full of numbers that promised their worst fears were impossible, or worse, that our fearlessness was empirically incorrect.

Doesn't 'having your head in the clouds' and 'having your head buried in sand' mean the same thing?

We're careening around a narrow road, posted up with streetlamps, and I'm watching a row of swans sit unanimated on a dark and virulent pond.

I am not among the living.

That's how Rasputin predicted his own death. At this point he's got me hooked, this self-absorbed professor from Dartmouth, who was drinking red wine on a plane.

"How can sin be erased without sincere repentance? And sincere repentance only comes after one has sinned." A preacher who justified sin with circular logic built his church and named it the Holy of Holies, a delicate sobriquet that belies the reality of it, the whores and sycophants sprawled along the floors, the raving drunks, parishioners kissing the feet and lips of their new Bacchus. Rasputin cured hemophilia in a young prince. He drank and womanized.

He claimed that he held the fate of Russia in his fist. Confidant of the Red princess, a gnarled old man with moss-like hair, streaming off his knotted and oaken head like a prehistoric tree, the fork-tongued peasant whispering sweet everythings into the Tsaritsa's blushing ear.

This is the part that really got me. When he was finally proclaimed dead, Rasputin's body was set to funeral pyre, but amateurishly prepared.

"See," the scholar says, running fake knives through the air with his fingertips, breaking into a fine sweat, "you need to sever the tendons and ligaments at crucial joints."

He almost tips over his wine, gesticulating like a conquistador. Stopping at times to remold his Vandyke. An unopened pack of kreteks on the foldout tray.

"The elbows maybe, and at the knees. You know, you have to do this to keep the muscles from contracting rapidly when they heat up. An incision across the lower back."

He says that's exactly what happened to Rasputin. He was improperly cut and when he was placed on the stack of wood and set to flame, he jumped out of the fire.

He came springing back to life.

Rasputin.

Almost reborn by God in a farmhouse cellar, then almost poisoned and shot to death in a dungeon. From a stone womb to a stone mausoleum. Beaten bloody and sent to die with his brother and sister under the river. Two infanticide merchildren, swollen and waterlogged, white shirts swelling around them like the paraffin layers of a jellyfish; bloodshot eyes. Then dragged from the river, jaunting erect while burning at the stake, the last shrieking cry of the Siberian phoenix.

Alright, let me tell you a funny story.

I was at home on a four-hour layover, visiting my mother. She was outside digging a hole with a splintery garden pick and I was watching from a lawn chair drinking unsweetened iced tea.

When the hole was around three feet deep, she bent the rigid, lifeless body of our dead cat, Merlin, into a shape that would fit the void. She draped a white shroud over him, placed him into the recess gently, then picked up a handful of dirt, which she sifted through her fingertips.

She was crying.

I guess this story isn't that funny. Funny like, topical, I meant.

I gave her a long hug, and shoveled back the dirt as she walked, trancelike, back inside the house. I could see her through a window, sitting on a rocking chair in the dark. I patted down the soft earth, a bald spot on our otherwise lush front lawn. Craned over by sunflowers. A few of our other cats walked over. Cats at a cat funeral, pawing around.

I took a sip of iced tea.

I stood back and wondered, which would you rather? Death as a human, and all of the black clothes that come along with our awareness? To be a part of the only species that wears veils? The privilege of grief, the sophistication to mourn? Or quick animal death?

You should see the way a cat's tail just curls around like a question mark, spry off the end of its body like an antenna, the way its nose wrinkles up when it walks over its sister's grave.

Would you rather be poisoned, shot, or drowned?

"Not anymore," I answered quickly. "The probability of getting in two airplane accidents in one lifetime is beyond microscopic. It's laughable really."

So I tell him this.

I tell him I was twelve-years-old flying from Baltimore to Chicago and it was snowing heavily at Midway. We hit the ground and slid like a toboggan. We kept going. Down the runway. Off the runway. Through fences, streetlights, electrical wires.

You may have seen it on the news.

I tell him, "You know what I can't get out of my head? The look of the thing."

Watching it later on television, thinking, how preposterous does it look to have this tremendous orange and blue aircraft nosing into traffic? Just this bulbous front end, bellied up on the highway like a beached whale.

"I mean, just, sitting there." And then I realize that I'm crying.

You may have heard about this on the radio.

"Are you afraid of flying?" I ask.

"Hell," he gulps, restarts, "Heck no I'm not."

"Tell me your worst story," I say.

And he tells me this:

He says a guy gets a call, says both of his parents had a stroke in their nursing home, to come quick.

Haven't we all heard stories like this before?

So he throws on a button-up shirt, or a pullover, or maybe he does go with the button-up but he only buttons it halfway.

"I only say it because every second matters."

The guy gets in his car, doesn't check his mirrors, and tears down his block. He's driving too fast. Way too fast even. He blows a stop sign. Then another. And on the third stop sign . . .

This guy I'm sitting with, he pauses here for what seems to be a long, long time.

Then he claps his fist into his palm.

"Wham!" he says. "T-bone."

And guess who's in the car? Just guess that it's his parents in the other car. Of course it is, we've heard these types of stories before.

"So whose parents had a stroke?"

Someone else's. McRae's not Mackay's, or however it went. They called the wrong number. At the desk, they dialed an eight instead of a damn nine. And what were Mackay's parents even doing driving around? Visiting their son, of course. Or going to visit him.

"What's the fu—" He scratches his beard. "What's the chances of that?"

I tell him I didn't know. I say, "That's not my type of statistic."

People who say that when you die, your soul comes floating from your body, a glowing angelform, rising through the ceiling, looking back down—I think those people are wrong.

My driver turns into the driveway sharply, stopping an inch off the bumper of my grandfather's station wagon.

When you die, your body bursts into a black cloud. It billows out of your windows like a house on fire. Creeps up the chimney like ivy. Great black tendrils scrawling skywards. A black plant colossus, thorny legs rooting into your front yard. Something you can see from far away.

The bad aura.

He says nothing, but rolls up the divider between us.

I get out and run up the stairs to the front door. The scene plays out scratchy through the screen door. My grandfather, leaning my grandmother off his knee like they are doing some saturnine tango, screaming for help, the driver slowly lifting my bag out of the backseat, whistling while chanting,

"I am no longer among the living."

Then my grandmother's eyes roll back in her head, my grandfather's eyes fill up blue with tears, I get this rushing scent of childhood, and now I'm shaking, a cat roping around my grandfather's leg.

THE DARK HEAT.

Madeleine's got a heat between her knees. Well, that's the way her dead mom had always phrased it after her signature morning dirty. (A prayer now, for our dearly, drunken departed.) That tongue loosening cocktail of course partially contributory to her untimely demise; the chances of finding her without glass firmly in hand about as good as finding the Statue of Liberty without her torch.

Maddy's always classified her drinking a little differently. Palliative, calming, and (importantly) always mixed with juice. And Daniel would never get furious with her the way Dad used to with Mom, during those martini evenings in the nightmare 1980's, "Days of Our Lives" always sort of blaring in the background.

So we've got our protagonist, progeny of a mechanic and an intermittently-employed drunkard. Typical enough ingénue, who is a just another parcel of damaged goods working in the financial sector; but is the story just that simple? Despite the hyper-red lipstick and the legs crossed at the ankle and the cigarette tucked just so into the over-red lips and the chip like even faintly visible on the daintily spaghetti-strapped shoulder? We tune in and reserve judgment momentarily. Despite the come-hither stink of Camel Light smoke and Chanel N° 5. Despite some of the more subtle warning signs.

What could be happening to young Madeleine that's so captivating we're willing to dismiss these little ventures in stereotype? Here's a quick checklist. Cheap jewelry and lightweight outfit, streamlined and stripped of material in the décolletage, equipped standard w. high skirt-line + built-in with optical illusions of eye-narrowing hourglass print and vertical pinstripes, and an orchestrated snugness and with some aftermarket excisions too that enhance the key elements- bawdy, piscine, windowed, a check, check, check.

The drink itself, an Appletini, is an homage to the wreckage of prenominate mother figure, a somewhat diluted heirloom, maybe, but indicative of a shared root cause, finished before the conical glass even gets a chance to lose its frost. But it must be more than just these factors that've led to Maddy's problematic management of interpersonal relations. Hermès scarf, check. Louboutin heels, check. And a coolness of head and a muscular calm that speaks to some high-profile pharmacological connection. No. She knows a boat's crew worth of girls who do just fine for themselves and have dependencies on wildly higher price tags, proofs, and numbers in milligrams. For more insight, we consult her telephone, laying face up on the round bar table next to a candle (lit), except it's only Daniel, back at home, and he's simply worried, up so late, himself doing some consulting, consulting the driveway minutely, even though Madeleine's Carrera keeps not coming.

This laundry listing of luxury items grows tiresome. Do you know who would be most tired with all of this name dropping? Do you know that Alex MacGregor, M.D., tall, dark, handsome, currently approaching from the northwest, would take least kindly to such an egregious verbal carpet bombing of words and phrases that convey wealth and status? One Alex MacGregor (M.D.) whom friends almost universally refer to as 'Mac,' who is now folding a hand-me-down blazer over the barstool adjacent to the barstool currently occupied by Madeleine, who is making an earnest attempt to stop giving herself so many backhanded compliments.

But why is he here? And why is our heroine, normally so taut and composed, doing this delicate shake like a tree limb in a storm wind, and why is she reaching so frequently for her drink? Most readers will cite the sedative properties of alcohol. Are we supposed to read all sorts of congenital connotations in her using cold vodka as a social crutch? And if so, is the mother rolling in her grave or giving a soft, postmortem applause? This is supposed to be Zithromax's job. Isn't this why we've got Dilaudid?

Maybe it's something about Mac. Definitely not too far a stretch. Mac: dashing, hirsute, broad-shouldered, not *too* unlike his television counterparts. But there's a new intensity to him tonight, a sort of smoldering focus, and our young Madeleine is the ant to his magnifying glass. Mac's no sadist! Though even he'd admit, it felt *nice*, shoe being on the other foot, Maddy @ a rare loss. Before we back up into the ancillary roughage, to dig up some expository detail on these two, let's move a little closer to the hole. The diffraction pattern on the bar napkin under her drink, the little tectonic chips in her French manicure, which meant she was biting @ her fingernails again, the periorbital hyperpigmentation around her eyes a sure signifier of some late nights.

Mac had a strong handshake and a 12 handicap and didn't wear cologne. Didn't need to.

Now let's back up for a second. Maybe spare you all the story of how these two met and just, instead, highlight a few times they deviated from the nauseating romantic norm. What's probably most important is that Madeleine is not sleeping with this man. That much is true. And they were conducting their affair in some non-standard locations. If you could even call it an affair. They avoided the hotel rooms and dimly lit annexes of out of town bars that are the stock locales of so many a plainer romance. At least, they avoided them before tonight.

Though, come to think of it, their origin story is actually worth mentioning. They met in the hospital once when Daniel's seismic fucking life event had been downgraded, first from full blown cardiac arrest to something more minor, and again to a "ventricular episode," two floors up from the emergency room, and then again, in some more lightly traversed west wing of the sick bay, declassified to simple angina, a hypochondriacally-provoked bout of coughs, or caffeine abuse, or sloes, or La Grippe, or foul humors, or whatever. Madeleine first saw Mac drinking from a water fountain next to a potted plant and a soft bench outside of Daniel's hospital room like some sort of Norman Rockwell painting come to life. Except in some bizarro-Americana where everyone wants badly to fuck one another.

Although even now I feel like I'd be remiss to not point out that Daniel and Madeleine and even Alex "Mac" MacGregor are operating under pseudonyms. But who could blame them? No one likes being exposed in their (alleged) affairs or accused of faking an illness for their own personal gains. When Alex was first confronted with the notion of using an alias he bristled, confident as he was (and still mostly within his rights, as he and Maddy hadn't even fucked, after all.) Mostly though his objection was with the terminology. *Nom de plume* meant pen name, and they were no writers. Alias made him feel like he was C.I.A. or in the witness protection program. And he was in no rush to make this seem any more serious than it already was. *Nom de guerre* has been imbued with such a high dosage of snark over the years that it seems almost universally unusable. Cognomen, agname, agnomen, pseudonym. Even the words themselves sounded nasal and phlegmy and duplicitous. They tried choking you up as you tried to pronounce them, like they were trying to stop you from using them. And then Mac realizes that maybe he's been parsing and scrutinizing and over-analyzing this topic just like he had been parsing, scrutinizing and over-analyzing every side and facet of the relationship dice he'd rolled since basically the get-go.

What was it about this girl?

We should mention here again, Daniel, like a puppy at the window of the second story apartment that he shares with Madeleine, doing a similar amount of over thinking. Here he is, vibrating with worry over some stacked or heaped or trowelled out portion of dessert and its accompanying goblet of Nero d'Avola. Because, though Daniel was no whipping post, he was also not a complete stranger to grief. He was aware of certain endorphin-producing qualities in chocolate. And he paired certain wines with different emotional states: dinner with old friends, engagement announcement, Bat Mitzvah, a perfect spontaneous *a cappella* song harmonization, post-relationship misery, Dutch edam, artful seduction, grateful reciprocity is, respectively: Cabernet Sauvignon, Pinot Noir, Manischewitz, box of unnamed house red, Nero d'Avola, Gewürztraminer, Chardonnay, Chianti. When the E.R. doctor asked Daniel if he drank (alcohol) he said only days when he was "off." Off from work? That's up to only us to guess.

So what of the alleged heat between Ms. Madeleine's stockinetted knees? Crude offhand conjecture of an aging, perennially unfulfilled housewife (with a drinking problem) or valid psychosexual critique from the woman with maybe sole authority on the inner workings of Maddy's heart comma soul?

Mac could wager a guess. Though right now, Mac seems tilted, disappointed, possessing of a dreadful, burdensome secret and a cindering gaze but squinching a little with every sip of his Manhattan. MacGregor (alias), medic extraordinaire, previous serial heartbreaker, is a machine not built for whiskey, God Bless Him. His capabilities are ranged but lie elsewhere. So why this girl? Why change everything for this girl? It seems unlikely that it's because of any metaphorical rise in temperature between patellas. And it doesn't read like your typical pregnancy scare. Madeleine recipient of, let's put it gently, some preemptory medicinal safeguards, scattered in amongst the anxiolytics. And secondly, they'd never even *had sex*.

So explain the bed of moisture in Mac's generally desiccant and surefire palm, or his correspondingly moist brow? One last word on Madeleine maybe. It's necessary to point out that her ability to love (and be loved) had not been completely exfoliated by the rough touch of an abrasive maternal influence. Madeleine wasn't too far gone, not yet. So if she's not a complete tragedy, then what? Why did this keep *happening*?

The bar's lined with swamp lights, the cocktails are Molotov, dark animator bartender death merchant, coasters: toe tags, jukebox scherzo dirge a là Chopin; you can almost see Mac and Madeleine (aliases) doing a little conjoined tailspin into depression like, where to go from here but screaming headlong into the scene of the crash? Chinks in the parental armor have been recognized, aired out. Possible chemical influences on board but not with hands on the helm. And so Madeleine considers herself, justly maybe, an of-age female human in working condition, receptive to the idea of quote-love-unquote, and prides herself even particularly capable of taking it as well as she dishes it out. But could we just stop and consider this from her side for a second? On the one hand, she's got Daniel. Loving, a provider, warm, good listener, traditional; a well-worn favorite. On the other hand something of an intellectual beast, shades there, of genius, a professional, statuesque. Two chutes though, equally as long and slick and dark.

But none of what you've read here is real. All of the names have been changed. Any resemblance to real persons, living or dead, is purely coincidental. Or, that's what she hoped. That despite the heat, and his dark stare, and Daniel off somewhere alone, that maybe this wasn't happening. This is what she hoped and hoped and hoped.

DOWN THE OLD BEND.

Last light is perfectly indistinguishable from first light, down the old hull-curve bend that follows the coastline. The truck's just a muted blip of cream colored paint and a red stripe as he accelerates a little into the turn, into a soft play of sun, and so he tips the visor down as he drives roughly into the direction of the fogbow.

Four stop signs holding their secret grudge in a winter field; forming a rudimentary windrose with their backs turned. Adam closes his eyes. A long, long blink. A swollen plane of crabgrass, a red house with striations of silver thaw high up on the hill, a left at the fork. He doesn't see these things. But there is a firm element of trust- between Adam and the car, the car and the road.

A firm trust in distance with relation to speed.

All Adam sees are the red dots skipping jubilantly on the back of his own eyelids. And he feels that warm feeling, registering somewhere deep in the skull, because the visor doesn't catch and block all of the incoming sun.

Then the white rocks dug into Murphy's front lawn.

Then the graveyard. Iron-hooked, mossy. Gravestones praying slowly towards the earth with time. A population of old rock, fenced-in, sweetly scripted with old dates. Governed by the old grave keeper, who takes his nights in the church. Adam can picture these things because he knows they are there. When the long blink is over, he is sitting properly at a stop sign.

There are no other cars on the road.

Adam is driving now through the rainbow spume, water upshot and diffracted by its collision with roadside beach rocks, sun doing its chemical painting. He's heading to the bar, as per tradition for men in this town after a long day's work. He feels the vibrative friction of his accelerator. The bar's called Sexton's Hideaway, but you'd be hard pressed to hear anyone refer to it as anything besides 'the bar.' There are gulls in the air and their shit on the rocks.

Adam pulls into to the bar parking lot slowly, approaches his usual spot, and digs his grill into a bank of dirty snow that looks like streusel topping. In a month or so, the front of his car will be outfitted with the large yellow snowplow that he keeps in the shed outside his house. But for now it's just the bare receptor fittings of the mount kit. His tires, splattered with mud, work themselves into the white mass.

Adam throws the truck in park and his exhale is visible as it curls and catches the glass of the front windshield, gaining physical life in condensation. Adam unbuckles. He opens the door and steps out. Adam stretches- a big, exaggerated pandiculation like someone greeting morning in a commercial for antidepressants. He stares windward, squinting at the sky, which was creamsicle and textured towards the horizon, blank and puckered-in towards the part you'd aim a cannon at, a sort of cottonball-brigade gloom high up overhead, which looked too orderly and mathematical to be made of clouds.

The bar has a channeled tin roof for sluicing ice and water, and a weatherbeaten wooden exterior that looks like an old brunette's hair going gray. A porch wrapped all the way around, more like something you'd find on a house. And for good reason. Sexton's *was* a house as recently as forty years back, when it was Old Marge's house. But then Old Marge passed, as old ladies are wont to do, and her nephew Guy gutted the place out, and put in new storm windows, and built a bar.

That same handmade bar sat there still, cocked about five degrees atilt, as Adam comes walking through the front door, pulling off gloves.

Around back, Adam knows, there is a dirt path that connects greyly to another dirt path, a branch that schoolchildren have sort of ground out through the years, and this path connects also to more dirt paths, the lot of which form a sort of communal dirt path nexus that feeds most of the nearby stores. And one of these dirt thoroughfares brushes tangentially, by means of another dusty rivulet, with the dirt path that leads to the back door of the old church on Windsor Street, terrestrial precursor of sorts to the aforementioned graveyard.

And so the name of the bar wasn't completely arbitrary after all.

The bar itself is a full square, its wood chipped and etched, and Guy's doing the Sunday crossword somewhere near the medial point in one of the square's sides; dead-set between two counters upturned on their swinging hinge-joints.

The liquor here shows strong partisanship towards the brown.

Only two or so beers on tap and so then the rest of the row is just empty screw ports with no handles.

A statue of Gambrinus in the nook above the register, glowering avariciously down at his sotted acolytes.

Meryl the waitress now taking inventory with a worn down yellow pencil.

A ship in a bottle behind Meryl, whose installment was lobbied for by Mutton Senior, seen twice here now by Adam, due to the bar mirror's reflection of it.

Adam takes off his coat and eschews the coat hanger in favor of sitting on the damn thing since the bar stools in here are craggy and have the consistency of frozen rock and so everyone generally crafts makeshift seat cushions out of their own jackets and coats.

Darts, craps, and toad-in-the-hole in the back, the fireplace and letterbox marina-view on the side, where a few sad dinghies swish obediently on their hawsers.

Was he dreading his sister's visit?

Not in the classical sense.

Adam knew what she was here for, and he felt something like a prorogued judge, awaiting trial. But Adam knew mostly what it was she'd come to say. This was not a dynamic that sat completely right with him. All of a sudden he's the one with leverage, the one with gavel-in-hand. He had no interest in being plied. This all reminded him of why he'd come up here in the first place, to escape situations exactly like this. To vertically transcend emotion. She was due in tomorrow, and represented a potential overdose of the past. And Adam loved his sister, he did. But she was the first mate taking that long, grave walk to the bridge, to inform the captain that the ship was sinking. He already knew the deal. And nobody likes bad news.

Adam sits down, feels some of the cold leaving his body. Across from him is the well-labeled rectangular panel of light switches that correspond to different areas of the bar: the side patio, the annex, the stained-glass over the pool table, the string lights that border the bar mirror.

To the direct right: the glass frame of the liquor license, which is cracked in two places, and is surrounded by a pastiche of goodluck dollars, one old Québécoise piastre. Down the eye-line, only a few of the liquor bottles have speed pourers affixed, the majority are wrapped up in shrink wrap.

It's one of those bars where they keep the cups hanging upside-down in a rack, like sleeping bats, ready to absorb the tap's blood. The architecture of the rack actually very intricate, the throat of it an o-slot which winnows back towards the distal and proximal ends, the stems of the glasses received in the middle and then caught soundly in the taper. Adam happens to know this was all "Tall" Dean Begum's handiwork, a commissioned piece—Guy and him'd worked out a deal wherein his minor carpentry know-how was employed in exchange for a week's free bar tab.

Dean's sitting in here now, as he does, next to the Mutts. Arnold Maciejewski Sr. and his son, Arnold Maciejewski Jr., look like the two sides of those police composite photos they draw up when a young person goes missing. There were some thickened elements in the senior Maciejewski, in his beer gut, in the lenses of his glasses. And some thinned elements too, in his more lightly golden and thinned-out hair, in his skin that looked more like rice paper. They were both called "Mutt," and collectively "the Mutts," abbreviations both of the word "Mutton," which was the nickname of the first Arnold Maciejewski to set foot on American soil, as the Maciejewskis were butchers in the old country.

No one here seems particularly thrilled to be drinking. It seems to Adam that there is an inverse relationship between the age of a person and the amount of fun that person has in bars. There's a tipping point, though he doesn't know at what age, where the bar starts having fun with *you*.

Adam's always had a sweet affection for old bars with some sort of idiosyncrasy, hiccup, or routine. Sexton's Hideaway's inside joke is the hot water heater. And if you've been here more than once, you're in on it. The responsibility cycles among regulars.

There is a noise.

The noise happens sporadically and without warning- a bad transmission shift noise, that of cog versus gear, followed by an almost human-sounding belch. The ensuing silence meaning *someone* is up to bat, and has to go and fix the heater. The lineup was written down once somewhere, but has been long since memorized.

And wouldn't you know it?

The damn thing breaks. And since the list does sit firmly in the group's collective memory, no one stands up. It's Guy the bartender's turn, because *nemo est supra legem*. So Guy slaps a bar rag over his right shoulder and then off he goes, in all his flannelled glory, oaken torso bobbing arhythmically thanks to a hitch in his giddy-up that he's had since just about exactly the time he was shipped home from the first Gulf War. Adam watches him descend towards the heater's sanctum. Inside a shuddered back-compartment lies the octaploid monstrosity, an old steampunk rig outfitted with accordion gills and tubular blackcopper tentacles, which chug animatedly in its dark corner.

Here's the modus.

Step 1: Find the light switch. Guy finds it quickly, as most of the more experienced guys do, though drinks play a hand in this process throughout. **Step 2:** Find a matchbook. There are generally a few laying around, on the wooden ledge or some other jut in the infrastructural framework. Having to come back to the bar for a fresh pack warrants jeers, faux-applause. **Step 3:** Hit the match and guide it towards the pilot. Many bar patrons lose interest at this point, back rapt into their ponies or seasonal ball games. But Guy can bank on some fresh Hell from anyone still clued in for every match he can't get to strike. **Step 4:** (And here's the tricky part…) Feel out the gauge. Tricky insomuch as if the dial's set too high the match'll torch out, and if it's too low, the hot water heater will sink right back into its drudgery and insolence, as the heater itself has no personal interest in the comfort level of the patrons, and prefers, maybe, its latent state. **Step 5:** Tap the old beast thrice on its flank, an ancient protocol of unknown origins that earns you a free drink, always, at the bar. Which makes the whole routine worth your while, sort of, as if you had a choice.

No such incentive for Guy, really.

A lexical gap; Adam was looking for a word somewhere between talent and habit, wherein he'd narrate out of someone else's head sometimes. When he was drunk enough, he'd do it out loud, and received mostly warm receptions. Now though he's doing it internally, and it's Murphy's brain that's cherry pink and split open down the middle on the operating table. The vowel differentiation of the Old Irish and a buckshot of apostrophes denoting the elisions. Otherwise, Adam's best approximation:

Mug a joe 'n' me whiskey, sure. All I need. 'Ese b'ys 'ere eat cherrystones like they were 'tater chips. Horvath was borderline sociopathic, wa'n't he, when they gave him his license? Only now I ain't have two nickels even to rub together. Southern folk'd rather go ta that damn greasetrap down the freeway, kitchenbell always ringin' and the pinball makin' a' racket. Though a' course, that takes the quarters, not nickels. As they say. Nice an' warm in here 'cept we ain't talkin' 'bout the waitresses. Ah! Meryl? Sailor's widows most of 'em. Fat now 'n' chaste 'n' bitter 's lemons. Frigid 's the gull shit on a metal roof.

That's something Murphy would say, Adam kept to himself, amused, as Guy returns to the bar, amidst mild applause, for his quick performance, a veritable pro with the fucking thing.

Next:

"Tall" Dean Begum orders a 'cup of the quiet.'

"Better make it two," Adam says. Then he tries to remember. He thinks it was the senior Mutt who started calling his whiskey 'the quiet.' Adam always sort of treasured that little epithet, *the quiet*. Short form version, he romanticized, of: what'll quiet your mind, what'd put you quietly to bed.

Adam and some of the other boys head outside for a smoke.

A light drunk already taking form, growing mouths. Some of them start talking about their former lives. Adam plays coy about his history "down south." There are a hundred thousand things these grizzled men do not know about Adam the Greenhorn. Sort of a frosty tide, that catches and half-drags off the piers, leaving icy beards on the bollards and dock posts. A trim of icing around the crab lines, white outlines on the cobalt breakers and an archery of cold wind that pierces through spaces between shirt buttons, gaps in scarves. These men are career laborers. They've logged countless industrial hours. Adam makes vague head-nod agreement analogues at all mentions of the drudgery inherent to brute labor and physical toil. These northern fishing jobs were dead ends in the most literal sense. This is where geography ran out for these men. Men who chased their dreams or, more often, escaped their nightmares, by taking the northward plunge. And the other faction, working alongside the émigrés? Were the ensconced, generational locals. Men whose grandfathers and great-grandfathers had fished these same waters, and so had accumulated centuries-worth of old sea stories. Bred of dockhands and crabbers, raised by dockhands and crabbers, destined for dock-handling and crabbing, forever and ever, Amen. Men who lived off the fat of the sea, oblivious to the vastness of the larger world. Everything began and ended within a net's cast of their place of birth. Ambitions small enough to fit inside a lobster pot.

A stern and frigid air blows southeast, pirouetting the wind gauges, coming up off the water stiff and white-cold. A few schooners sliding home in the distance. Whitecaps in succession on the beach. Adam having trouble with a pack of matches.

The quintet of cigarettes has a strange double-effect on Adam's judgment. His physical brain feels a little more cloddy and emulsified, but the voice of his rationale seems louder. It's time, he thinks, to maybe go home. He heads inside, a fresh beer's head slowly dying in a glass on the coaster in front of his chair, marked by his jacket, folded nest-like in the basin of its seat.

An hour passes. Maybe two.

Adam gauges his drunk on a ternary scale, as follows: 1) is sober, or close enough to it. A (1) means definitively good to drive. All clear. 2) Herein lies the only problem area. A (1) or a (3) are clear-cut decisions. The (2) is a nebulous middle ground that calls for reasoning and choice. Homebrewed field sobriety tests. Walking the trapezoidal concrete parking stops like tight ropes. The names of the streets in town, reverse-alphabetically. Field-tests administered by other drunkards. Yes, (2) is a gray area. But (3) is a no-brainer. Mutt Junior or Guy the bartender scoops you up from a (3) and shovels you into the backseat or flatbed of a pick-up and hauls you home, drooling, a bent philosopher, drooling but bargaining for another whiskey, demi-glace from the mouth up, like the last slow bits of a toy unwinding, fat charnel-house gibbous in the low, dead sky and the stars jitter and stretch, freezing white, when the truck hits a bump in the road. A (3) means a good night's sleep. There was actually a (4)th category, reserved for some truly legendary feats of drunkenness, a stratosphere Adam had yet to pierce, and, even though prevalent in occurrence in the oral lore of the bar, no one had attained such a ranking since Dean Begum did so on the last night of his free week.

Adam tries to avoid nights that end in (3)s. Tonight is just a (1). He leaves early, and waves goodbye, and the rest of the Sexton faithful don't seem to notice. The door shuts, and now it's just Adam and the huge ice-blue outside. Lot of black and stars bearing down. His blinks are long again. More dangerously so. He's walking across the parking lot. He's getting into his truck and driving. His drive is taken in some wide-shot angle; he's far removed from himself. He can feel the upgrade on South Drive, and so knows when to push the brakes. Knows Tully's laundry flapping on the line, knows the dead spigot, knows the antique Conestoga scenery wheel, knows this particular gulf of mold, of shale, of sea carve, of road, of one-story houses, of wind lines, of everything.

Even in the dark.

And then he pulls into his driveway, a worn out flare of dirt that showed through former grass, which was a testament to Adam's policy of never parking in the same exact spot twice. When he'd bought the house, the driveway looked more like a helipad than the single-file, stone-edged pavement projects of his youth. So he figured he would live into this liberty. When he came home and parked, he nipped at the grassy fringe. In great leafing evolutions, he'd expanded the driveway at the expense of his lawn; a fulminating star of dirt, each new cession a fresh angle to fit into and park, to say nothing about the more sovereign new ground broke on night's Adam came home (2) drunk to see.

So much space in between Adam and the next person who *knew* him.

He felt free.

He was the tree falling in a forest.

Two locks, and two corresponding keys on his front door, which made three counting the lock around back; by *far* the most in town.

Adam steps into his mudroom.

The mudroom was an absolute requisite on Adam's end during the bargaining and buying process of his home. The mudroom served a very specific and necessary process. Soon after Adam had moved in, he'd bought thick, blackout curtains to hang in front of all the mudroom's windows. Then he bought a towel rod like you'd hang in a bathroom and affixed it to the eastern wall. He bought one thick plastic mat like you'd find on the floorboards of an industrial truck and he laid it underneath the towel rod. He bought one sturdy, copper hook and screwed it into the slim slit of wall in between the windows on the western wall. The very specific facility of this mudroom was for full decompression. When he got in after a day's work he would strip down here, and he'd place his work boots, mud-splatted like the wheels of his truck, on the rubber mat. He'd unlock the portal door, which gave entrance to his home proper, but he wouldn't open it. Not until he'd taken off his shirt and hung it on the copper hook. And not until he'd undone his belt and taken off his pants, which were specked both with paint and eraser marks of cigarette ash and smelled like turpentine and cigarette smoke and exhaust smoke and different forms of earth. These he'd hang over the towel rod. Next he'd take off his socks and stuff them in his boots. He'd take off his underwear and fold them over once and either start a new pile on the floor else add them to a pile he'd already started on the floor which'd be brought inside for cleaning once a week. He placed the keys to the truck on a windowsill. By the time Adam worked himself inside his apartment he'd be completely naked and he would move directly into his shower.

He showers for exactly the length of time it takes to whistle the chorus of Green Sleeves three times over.

And so that's what he does, as he does, as people do what people do. After the shower Adam gets into loose shorts and a white tee shirt and pours himself a tall drink. He finishes the drink and then pours himself another and when he finishes that he washes the glass and falls into a fugue state, apprehensive as he is but gelled down by scotch, grateful for the little interregnum nap to come. One last quietus of sleep separating his deserter's life from his sister's arrival. Wherein she'd come and mash things unnervingly back together. Then cajole or console him. Which one? He didn't know. But either way she was about to make this whole thing so agonizingly real.

Adam wakes up well before noon and decides he'll go out for a walk. To try and steel over his nerves before she gets here. It was a mechanism of his, walking to clear his head, something as ancestral and homeopathic as he could imagine. Adam walks down his driveway, etched out like a pine tree in reverse, his hands buried firmly in his pockets. A plucky cold. He works his way through residentia, towards thicker town. The town itself was swept back, salted over. Halite and chromefrost fittings in all parts of the scenery, draft-stopper clad and thoroughly caulked homes heated by woodburning stoves, the proof in cords and stacks on pitched hills in various backyards in front of cold suns, axes worked picturesquely into stumps. A birdfeeder community, a craft & book store town, cobbled on top of rock, frozen solid together. Adam phases through town and to the upper seawall. He descends, over rocks, to the beach. The breakers were looking a little pitched and urgent, with whitecaps, and some blackness over the swell: an easily readable stormglass. Adam kicks off his boat shoes and buries toes into cold sand. And that's where he stayed for a long time, transfixed in that ageless and answerless vacuum of sea gazing. The repeater of waves and waves and waves giving their maddening effect. He thought about navigators of old. Great and ambitious men. Men who did not shy from destiny. How simple it must have been to stare across an ocean and wonder what was on the other side. And wonder how best to get across. But what's left to fantasize about now? Now that everyone else has got everything so figured out?

A quick word on his sister Hayes. Adam had always chalked up his normal-sounding name to some sort of parental imperative, whereafter committing to some daring on their firstborn's name they'd played it safe on the sophomore run. Hayes and Adam's first names had strangely prophetic influences on their eventual personalities. Adam had always played the mute. Adam was the anonymous secondary. They'd named her Hayes, after the 19th President of the United States of America. This too had played to form, that odd name. It worked for her in that she had all the assertion, ambition, self-possession and aggression you'd imagine would be necessary in becoming president.

He walks back home, through puddled landscape and, back inside, he awaited her arrival.

Though briefly he indulges himself in one quick trip through Hayes' mind, as she pulled into his driveway. (Interesting he thought, that she did not pull up behind him but in a glancing alignment, **NEbN** and **NWbN**, in relation to his truck.) She would've had a lot of time to think, during the drive up. This is what Adam figured she'd said internally to herself:

"I won't cry. That's what I won't do. I'll do anything but that. I took the right steps. But even if you are well-pressed, and presentable, and prepared- disaster still comes and strikes. Even if you've memorized the required lines. Even if you measure twice before every cut. Even if you know the proverbs like the back of your hand. Work hard. Live clean. Live diligently and austerely. Live without any excess of sin or caprice, that ragged cloth which calamity clings to, on lesser and less sharply tailored human beings. You tried your best. Which they say is the best that you can do. But if you tried harder, maybe you

could've pre-supposed. No. Don't let this make you cry. Don't let him see you cry."

Hayes gets out of the car, wearing something summery and polka-dotted, that looks almost ultraviolet against the morning. She's a shine on darkened pewter, because the sky is grim and closing down and the color of a sea storm. A chainmail mesh of sparrows visible, darting between a gap in dreadnought clouds. Adam now feeling the sting of mockery weather sometimes impresses upon circumstances.

-Watch out!

The weather too clearly prescient. Hayes was strange at the front door. Embracing the gravity of the situation, brother and sister didn't fake an overblown or even cordial salutation. The door opened slowly, and there she was, of course she was, and so she sort of just moved past him, with only a momentary transference of warmth, a hand placed on his forearm, which was still affixed to knob, and then she's through the mudroom and into his living room, seeming all the more upset for being there.

The living room is spotted with vestigial miscellanea from Adam's past. Their importance won't be lost on Hayes. There's a cardinal red *Die luft* flag pinned fast into the wall. A trophy necklace in the standard goldenrod and maroon, with its navy tongue, fastened to a silver medallion. A photo of the two of them, happy looking.

All along it was Hayes who had been most let down by Adam's flight. Hayes had felt most particularly in tune with the capacity of Adam's full potential. And so she was doubly hurt by it all. All of these relics of his former life, so innocuous seeming, such background noise to his new buddies- they were sharp little daggers to Hayes. They were souvenirs of wounds past. An old jersey. A High School yearbook. Adam was picking up on it, watching her head parakeet around the room in survey. Watched the pricks of disappointment in her face like an emotional EKG. Hayes felt a quick cutlass of vicarious guilt, as she looked over the photos on the wall. Adam didn't have any photos of their brother. And now he's gone so too late now.

White rain comes sheeting over the house. Falling the way it normally falls, in great cuffing slants. Hayes takes a seat by the windowsill, watches it come down. Adam is familiar with it, the little percolating cauldrons of rain forming in the bucket windows and in the pitted-out pots of mud. The artillery on Hayes' hatchback mimics the sound of rainfall on his truck. Though in two different keys. And of course Adam's already heard the news. Hayes is sitting in a way that suggests she doesn't think Adam knows the news. A professional fold to her body, arms and legs set neatly like a dinner table, crossed the way a doctor might sit before he tells you that it's cancer. But Adam knows. He does. Bad news travels quick. And the reason he hadn't reached out is because this is the way he takes bad news. In isolation. They ought to know that. All of them. But she ought to know best.

A whalegray blanket of pins falling neatly onto the eastern side of the house.

"You're going to come?"

"Of course I am."

"It's not so of course."

"Of course I'm coming."

"It's Wednesday and Thursday."

"I know when it is."

"I'm just saying."

"Well I'm just saying I'll be there."

"I believe you."

"She sent you up here to make sure?"

"No one sent me to do anything."

"Sure seems like it."

"We knew you'd come."

"How could I not come?"

"That's what I said."

"She still doesn't trust me."

"I don't think it's that."

"What else could it be?"

"Yeah, well. Mom."

"I will be there."

"I know you will be."

"Good."

"Okay."

Hayes' M.O. is having it under control. It's funny almost, seeing her squirm here under uncertainty.

"You've been okay?"

"I have been."

"Good."

"You shouldn't worry about me so much."

"Why wouldn't we worry about you Adam? You're family."

"You worry about me *more*. You shouldn't worry about me more. Take care of your own worrying. Worry about your own worry."

This silences Hayes temporarily. So Adam puts himself at the funeral. He shakes those hands. He wears the black shirt and the black tie. He makes the sad faces. It makes him fucking sick. And here is Hayes, just about bursting at the seams. How badly, it looks, like she wants to bust and overflow into Adam, the composed and hieratic grim. But he came up here purposefully to freeze. He'd come up here and closed up emotional shop.

"What were you doing?"

"What?"

"When it happened?"

"Are you being serious?"

"That was a stupid question. You're right. I'm just so curious. I keep wondering if I'm going to keep remembering for the rest of my life what I was doing when it happened."

"What were *you* doing?"

"Watching television, I think."

"Well."

"Well what?"

"Who could blame you for that?"

"That's not it."

"If you say so."

"It's just that, I feel…"

"What?"

"Not *guilty*."

"Then what?"

"Just, curious I guess. Could I have been doing something different?"

"We all could've done a lot of things differently."

"But that day."

"That day probably not."

"So that's it then?"

"That's probably it."

"But what if not?"

Adam was at an ethical impasse. He had more to say, but he didn't feel particularly obligated to indulge Hayes' personal guilt. He knew the typical array of response. But he didn't feel up to delving into its different sectors. He didn't want to sound out the syllables of those scattered sympathetic platitudes. He won't say there was nothing you could have done. Won't be the author of those various, useless clauses. The myriad 'it's not your faults.' Like anything else, articulating things give them second life. Though he could feel this sentence lurking right up against the floodgate of blame. He began to think that Hayes' forthrightness in airing her own remorse was a form of subtle prodding. What she was saying, tacitly, was: 'even I am guilty.'

I feel guilty.

Now you feel guilty too.

A calm comes over Adam. He knows something that she doesn't know. In the time she's spent staying busy, hustling and gathering gear and foodstuffs for the ride up, in preparation for this dreaded conversation, Adam has spent coping- he has swallowed, digested and ultimately come to grips with excreting the horrible truth. He has passed the worst of it, prickly as it was, because they had been brothers like she never was. At the end of the day, Adam was certain that his heartache would always amount to more. Here he beats Hayes once. She was his superior in everything but grief. Hayes had her meteoric rip through school and college and career and marriage. Adam had this. Brotherhood. Deeper sorrow. A trifling little pyrrhic win for him, cradling a cup of the quiet in his neat living room as Hayes began to lose her self-control.

"You know. We did the morgue," she said.

Sort of a torrent of emotion in lieu of a response. This confirmed his dark suspicion. Here was that transference of fault he was waiting for. It was him they resented, Adam thought. This was survivor's blame.

But he did. He did go, was the thing. He'd been at that morgue every ensuing day of his goddamn life. Wasn't there in person. Didn't break through those swinging doors. Didn't get that printed name card or bathe in that fluorescent light. Breathe in the sick formaldehyde. Adam thinks, I didn't have any last words gurney-side but I've logged a hundred thousand conversations ever since. Ghost discourse. Signifier of mild insanity, he knows. But to say he wasn't there? That doesn't feel right. That isn't fair. He was there. He is there. He will be there, he imagines, in whatever subterranean room, in whatever coolly clinical stainless steel icebox, with the bodies, his brother's and everyone else's, forever and forever.

Hayes says she needs to rest up before her ride back home. So Adam makes the couch up for her and then heads out for another walk. It's only a mile or so down to the water. He takes the walk in a slicker because there's some residual spit. Some birds are back and cooing. Even this far away, even right outside his door, he can hear the tremendous shush and choke of water. There is a smell. He walks. And thinks. Everyone knows that time here was a broken clock. It was always raining or about to rain, or fresh off a rainfall, it seemed. It was almost always cloudy. And so this town kept time about as well as a sundial would, given the overcast conditions. Adam had never been too big a fan of the sun anyway. As he walks, he closes his eyes, and counts steps. Then the familiar creak of boardwalk. Then the familiar crunch of sand. He opens his eyes because the path is about to turn. The path feeds into the beach. Adam goes walking parallel to the shoreline, up in through the reeds, over some sedimental dunescapes. Adam closes his eyes again. Another length of beach travels silently underfoot. He knows the seashore's contours and can see its kelp-striped ridges, even with eyes closed, and knows somewhere deep osteological how the bands of broken shells get worked and lapped into lunar scrolls and knows by heart the make of the sandy crescents where multiplicate flagellum of waves lick repeatedly at the coast. In that huge blue hour before dawn he has, in the past, shrunk himself down real low, down into that granular mica, and he's felt himself get washed out, planktonlike, and he's gotten dug back up onto the wet beach, and there, prostrate and soaked, he's watched a huge white egg of sun crack itself open over stony breakers, and has felt his heartbeat blip in tidal sync with the red jettylights, and has breathed in, as the tide breathes in; a huge horizontal inhale and saline out-gush. And when he opens his eyes, he is here. He is wet and alive and here again.

There's a bed at home that's cold and military taut, suction-sealed against the wall, plush and near-impregnable and smelling lightly of fabric softener. Adam's always thought that the outside world would be unable to reach him there. He figured it just out of striking distance. Just far enough away. If maybe he could just stay asleep there forever.

Hayes left early in the morning, before Adam woke up. No surprises there. When Adam does get out of bed it's around **9AM** according to the wristwatch he keeps at his bedside table. He makes a pot of coffee and pours a mug of it and then looks out of the kitchen window, coffee mug in-hand. The sky was a cup of water fresh from the tap, the clouds vanishing like how the bubbles disappear. No surprises here either- it's another overcast day. Adam takes a lukewarm shower. Adam gets out of the shower and pours a cup of orange juice and drinks it and washes the glass and heads back into his bedroom, cold and haunted, and takes off his towel and hangs it on its designated rack. He finds socks. And underwear. And slacks. And a shirt. He sits for a long time on the end of his bed thinking about time and death and the nature of waves. When he's done, it's like he hasn't thought about anything at all. So then he heads to the mudroom. He puts on his jacket. He puts on shoes. And then he leaves for the door. He's got work to do.

THURSDAY.

Maybe we enter here, in media res, the sad man's sad palm attached to his small cock, in the shower, the water hot. And there's a silhouette one floor up, a gossamer partner in this pas de deux, a shadow at attention, in the moonlight, on a Thursday night.

After he comes he quickly snaps closed the curtain and then cleans up.

"Show's over, pal," the theatrical man says, to no one.

Flash forward to the next night at dinner: it's London broil and string beans, his favorite! (Or so thinks the wife.) In truth, he almost can't stomach this meal. But he'd been choking it down for so long that confessing to the lie would be even less palatable than slogging through the steak. Take a look at these dehydrated meats and waterlogged vegetables, metaphors both for her matrimonial concentration, he posits. Marriage and dinner. Two things she'd, technically, "accomplished," on paper and plates, officiant-stamped and ceramic respectively, but with results that were passable at best.

Also at the table is a six-year-old and a four-year-old. They are, historically, an alternating blend of frenetic and comatose. Together, they're a source of mild amusement but also trenchant guilt for this visibly woebegone man. To be clear, he loves them both dearly, as you do. But there's a part of him that sometimes imagines what it'd be like if they never existed at all.

The children are equally dissatisfied with the meal. Maybe they're vegetarians, the distant and uninformed man wonders. How do you tell someone you're a vegetarian before you've learned the word for vegetarian? He sympathized with the frustration bred by bad communication.

His beer tilts up and tries to find his face.

With little else to pride himself on, this particularly indignant man prides himself on his steadfast commitment to behaving indignantly. With conviction he refuses to eat; it is his silent protest. The wife doesn't seem to give a shit though, does she? She clears the table. She soaks the dishes. She loads the dishwasher. She pays no mind to however much food is left on the hungry man's plate when the meal concludes. But it turns out that this moderately overweight man is a secret, shameful eater. So, after putting on the hunger strike scene at dinner he supplements the lack of sustenance with late night snacks: takeout leftovers sheathed in flaked ice and bastardizations of Mexican fare and cheese ungodly canned and pizza corrupted in form-- what had ever been so problematic with pizza proper that impelled science to thrust it onto bagels and into pockets? Whatever the case, he'd become a nocturnal bon vivant of the freezer aisle.

These late night indulgences, however, would not be possible without an accomplice.

The microwave. That old enemy, his begrudging partner in crime. Long ago they'd engaged in some pyrrhic agreement wherein he'd feed it, and it would eat his shrink-wrapped and flavor-cinched and freeze-dried offerings, then regurgitate them back, its interior bloodstained where the canned ravioli sauce had, like lava, bubbled and popped. The microwave would duly gray his proffered meat, would liquefy the hungry man's presented solids, and then, when the man got back less than what he'd bargained for, he remained thankful. Thankful for the microwave's quick radiative magic; thankful at least for that black deed.

The morning after he is left with only his own gormandizing regrets. Had his stomach grown overnight? Maybe. He sits and wonders about this, like a strange, pale Buddha. Though atheistic. All the physical analogs, he thinks, none of the world-spanning spiritual reawakening.

In the morning, another shower. The lonely man turns the faucet on. In this handle, cold and stainless steel, he can feel the significance of angles. Can feel how even a slight deviation from vertex can create distance over time and over space. How subtle lists in radii and demeanor can derail marriages, see them skirring out of orbit, unlashed from the gravitational fields of nuptial vows.

The lonely but well-practiced man knows how far askew from dead center the hot and cold must both be to get the water right, because the lonely man has a lot of time on his lonely hands. At first, he had to stage a fixed experiment. The hot water was the control and the cold water was the variable group.

Oh, but that was such a long time ago.

A large untold variable in bathroom etiquette: how much clothes do you head into the shower with? Some undress prior but some strip down in situ. This dichotomy hadn't occurred to the ponderous man since high school. Back then, there were important homoerotic boundaries to preserve. Only now, when undressing in front of the wife seemed a mild antagonism, did being nude regain its stigmatic power. Being nude now was his venin little stratagem, tantamount to shouting: I dare you, I dare you to fuck me. But why? Why the uproar. Nudity, like many of life's depressing truths, was inevitable.

Once he does get naked he stares, at a scale that looks forlornly back at him like it wishes he wouldn't step. Don't make me deliver bad news, the scale seems to say. This sad, paunchy man sympathizes somehow with the unfeeling machine. He's not quite in the mood for bad news either. So he side-steps it. The scale, though straight-faced and blank and silver and chrome and un-activated, seems relieved to have not given him that added sorrow.

Then the lonely man clips his toenails. Not out of necessity but a sense of calendrical duty. He sits nude on the toilet and feels grotesque as he does it, all parts of the chore slick, fat, dirty and bunched together. It's why he always gets it over with quick, every first day of the month.

Eventually, he steps into the shower.

He likes the water hot to the point of not-so-mild dermic pain.

He starts the shower by sudsing up. Notice the word show built cleverly right into the word shower. In time, his stroke becomes slower; more ruminative. It's impossible to pinpoint the moment when the ostensible washing becomes masturbation. It is a fine line. There is an element of dramaturgy absent in his otherwise solo technique. And why shouldn't there be? This was somewhat of a production. There is an audience. There had been an opening night.

When using his showman's stroke he likes to linger around the tip like a man polishing a trophy. Lather begins to compile around the base of his cock, the fringy ends of pubic hairs making for good soapsud nucleation sites. He maintains a jazzy rhythm. He can feel the urethra running under the shaft like some sewage tube servicing a floating city.

At some point, the lonely yet diligent man must start rubbing the fog off the bathroom window, else the fog'd occlude the shadow's view.

He knows the shadow is watching.

He can feel him watching.

And then the man does what he both hates and loves to do: he comes. Another fossicked nugget of temporal gold in an interminable line of mud.

This is how the rest of his life unfurls. In the dreary space between orgasms:

Last summer, this solitary man had done a decidedly unsolitary thing. He'd packed the Astrovan like a Conestoga and braved the mountain passes separating suburbia and the nearest water park. The children, geeked up on their innate fearlessness of physical danger and general naïveté towards waterborne contagion, were thrilled.

The mysophobic man, well, not as much.

He disliked most of it. The chandelle of plasticized tubes, the slow reservoirs of epithelials, unclaimed piss and lost Band-Aids. The spray zones where sprinklers wet down the apoplectic toddlers in wet diapers increasingly likely to deposit their sodden contents onto the pastel-colored tarmacadam. Chunky Mesoamerican kids wearing white t-shirts that adhered translucently to their skin. Abandoned banshee children crying wild. Gearhead punks slinging down their preferred asymptotes, and then marauding across the fairways, trading high-fives and teen nomenclature, rattling around just about as un-self-consciously as possible, clattery and swaggering in their taut little physiques.

Something about people eating in their near-nude states made the man feel ill, eddies of melted ice cream pooling in roughed drains, all scents colliding and diffracting and moving towards their end death in chlorine. By late afternoon, tuckered out and woozy-of-head from so many drastic changes in elevation, the family capitulated to fatigue and tucked into a bird show, desperate for shade. The show was crowded, and it smelled like coconut custard and sunbaked vomit. The performer was a man in probably his late forties dressed as a cartoon pirate, cajoling the toucans and cockatoos and birds of paradise into performing simple assorted tricks.

The unimpressed man, hot of skin and sapped of strength, felt cooked and spent and introspective, and he simply could not imagine how the man in the pirate costume concealed his disdain. At work, it took every fiber of the man's physical being to not bury a pair of scissors in his boss' eye socket. And the man wasn't even forced to feign any of this absurd ingenuousness. Maybe it had all been amplified by the late sun, the horrid squawks from the collection of exotic and irritable birds, the comparative delight spackling the faces of the docile crowd. But the man remembered feeling sad and confused, wondering how someone could fake happiness so well. It seemed impossible. And it had stuck with him. The man thought it was the most horrible thing he had ever seen.

On the ride home, the kids and the wife both passed out, reddening from their long day in the sun like the Astrovan was a convection oven. And so for a while it was just the lonely man and the lonely road.

But quicker than those sun burns had even fully peeled, whatever gratitude or goodwill that had been bought by the trip to the waterpark had evaporated. The kids quickly returned to their former fury, the afterglow borne of good deeds rendered faded, and the banal chaos of indifferent self-interest resettled over the household, like old weeds wrapped back through the picked flowerbed.

Dinner tonight is spaghetti. The fat man and the kids unanimously hate spaghetti. It is one of their rallying points. They've told the wife, their mother, this many a time, with great vim and, at times, with great vitriol. Sometimes, the youngest tells the wife in an even plainer and more easily readable sign language: by upturning the bowl and scattering the hated pasta all over both the high chair's plateau and the floor beneath. Ha! No one likes it! The ill-timed man exclaims. Sometimes though, the rigors of life exclude all other culinary options for the worked and equally tired wife, and so, spaghetti it fucking was.

After tonight's spaghetti dinner, the man and the wife disinterestedly watch the news. The wife hates the news, the man knows; hates it for its monotone cataloguing of rape and house fire and butcher knives through the skull. But what the perspicacious man also knows, in all his perspicacity, is that what happens when that television blinks off, is worse.

Because television is a simple technology. Not the plenipotentiary it seems, to the sheltered, and the young, but a relay device, capable only of the secondhand. Outside of technologies, there was only and always nature. And in nature, there are plenty of ways to get killed in earnest.

Bears capture a significant portion of the public's imagination. Likely because they're one of the few murderous beasts you also sort of want to love. But they'll wash you down with a drink from Old Faithful and pick their teeth with your bones. And so then Yellowstone, from geyser to prismatic geyser, runs red with the blood of picnickers. Electric eels aren't even eels. They're fish. But no amount of taxonomic pedantry could argue with the electric reality; 650 volts transcend genus. Alligators have no natural fear of humans. And why should they? Before you drown, and well before you're eaten, alligators'll snap your vertebrae to smithereens in their tessellated vise. Did you know that hyenas lack all courtesy? If they've got you incapacitated, they'll begin to eat while you're still alive. Most predacious big cats will go for the jugular, they will gnaw and pin and strangulate, trying to suck their kill of air. But a jaguar? A jaguar is the psychopath with the butcher knife. Their teeth are so big they'll just sink them through skull, instead of wasting all that time.

But the most sinister of all? The sad man knew, by way of simile, was the tapeworm. A tapeworm slips in unnoticed, and through its stealth, kills you more horribly. It lives with you and feeds off of you in parasitic symbiosis. Eventually, you starve, and die.

The news was a pleasant bit of escapism in the end. Real life was the invidious bit. And he hates to be dramatic, but there were nights when the sad man found himself practically craving for the sweet release of a butcher knife to the skull.

No matter the clear dissatisfaction on display, the night always ends with an exchanging of the phrase: "I love you." It is a corollary of the old axiom that the married must never go to bed angry. As if this unfelt rehearsal of three weatherworn words could undo all the rest. But they said it nonetheless, every single night, as bedside lamps clicked routinely off.

But once the love is gone, saying "I love you" feels a little like birthing a slug out of your mouth. Like other lies, it sort of feels revolting on the tongue.

And so most nights end like that, a pregnant post-proclamation silence hanging over the bed like a sick voyeur. He can hear the transition of sounds that means she's passed from consciousness into unconsciousness. The miserable man begs for sleep, and when it finally comes, he's not even there to be thankful for it.

Having children, that horribly misinformed man had disastrously thought, could be their saving grace. Sure, it was the nuclear option. The procreative red button. Going for, as the irony would later provide ample entendre for, broke. But what choice did he have?

He is in the scene of a repeated crime: the kitchen.

The wife is there too.

He is thinking on a stool near this kitchen's island, that contemplative man, and his faculties of memory, if nothing else, remain firmly in place. He can remember when the eldest was born. He can remember looking at the ultrasound and can remember thinking that the way they formatted it made it look like a kidney bean getting smeared by a windshield wiper. No. It was the happiest day of his young life. They just don't get adorable until a little later, he amended his thought. The second one? The girl? Well, it had been born too, at some point.

And the children were a grace, truly, even if irreparable damage to their parent's relationship had already been done. They, the children, represented this notion that, even if the resigned man had all but quit, and hung up his proverbial cleats, that maybe some of his aspirations could still one day be met. Only, one generation down. The children validated the theory that, though the he may never be the impresario himself, he may yet create a virtuoso, a genius, or a captain of industry, and could thereby reap some secondary acclaim. He could be the architect of an august lineage. This was a lens. He could shift his worldview around this possibility. This was his beautifying lens.

Though who even knew about the fathers of geniuses, it now occurred to him. What if, because he was a simple and uneducated man, he was removed from the legacy element altogether? Who was Tesla's dad? No one knows. Likewise, he'd die unknown.

Which is not to say that becoming a father hadn't changed him. It'd changed him in that he'd become a father and he'd always thought that becoming a father would change him and he hadn't changed at all, and so, his idea of fathering had shifted significantly. It shook him to his core, while disrupting little to none of his daily behavior.

The children come in looking for sandwiches.

"What sort of sandwiches do you want?"

The lonely man asks, trying hard not to splice in swear words. Because what a boring fucking question. They are not old enough to subject themselves to the piquant or umami pleasures of the world. They are creatures that subsist on sweetness. Sweet little idiots. They don't know what it's like to have the ones they love the most spurn them, and scoff at them, and laugh at their naked bodies, and make translucent allusions to how bad they want to fuck the men in their morning yoga classes. Those lithe animals. As if the paranoid man didn't already fucking know.

Impatient about the sandwiches, the kids loudly flee the scene.

Though what even are the rhythms of filial duty? The man thinks. Day to day, diaper to diaper, school years to summers and back again; the quick progression from kindred spirit to adversarial adolescent, that treacherous little bit of heartbreak; and then the dependency regression.

It's like flying kites. We can only keep them away for so long, try as we might.

Some nights, it took all the drinks he could get his hands on just to quell the terrible thought of it. Sometimes, after long bouts of combative quietude lobbed against the televised news, and the newscasters and his wife, the disillusioned man would come to find that whatever beer he had laying around the fridge just wasn't enough to make him sufficiently drowsy for bed. So he'd run out for more. Kids fast asleep, he'd scoot out for another six pack, for soporific purposes only, of course. Admission to even sleep, nowadays, costs ten bucks.

Though he's not unhappy; not in the classical sense. Because, lonely and tired as he was, he was also bright enough to realize that loneliness in and of itself was not so terrible a pain in the grand scheme. But this comprehension of the human suffering continuum, and whereupon it he registered, proved an uncomfortable dissonance for the lonely man. Because a crude equation occurred to him. Murder victims suffer greatly, but momentarily. House fires, rape, butcher-knifings; these represent suffering at its piqued apex, undoubtedly. Victims of depression, however; they suffer languidly, and for such a long, long time.

An age old dilemma: a moment under the guillotine, or a lifetime on death row? Who could say what was worse.

Not this man.

This man's specialisms lay elsewhere:

This depraved man is a very special type of individual, he cares most especially about himself. Which means he leaves both friends and family in his masturbatory wake. Credit him this: He is majorly equitable in how he spreads the seed around. From his jerking's nervous preamble right on down to the sundown of post-coital tristesse he'll feel quilted in sexual remorse, but that, the guilty man knows, feels both good and bad at once. So in the interim he's golden; stroking and golden and invulnerable, and he'll gladly flay your daughters and your wives and the in-laws, strip them stark naked, submit them to his invisible will, hand-fast-to-palm. He'll be their masters just only for this one licentious moment. Then he'll silently ask you for your forgiveness. The shape of a Catholic gesticulation skewed forty-five degrees, his hands joined in tissue and his underwear still fettering together his knees.

How did it come to this?

Well...

They're both still sitting in their kitchen. Doing what? Almost nothing. Here's the wife, who showed all of the telltale signs of late-in-life ordinariness that you could've expected. It was the hopeful man, ever the Pollyanna, who chose to ignore these signs. He had hoped, like dumb and hopeful men do, that the sunny personality would never fade. But guess what? The light and lissome in women are vulnerable traits. Just like the trim and debonair are in men. We're all on a slick cline, the man knows, towards paunchiness, and baldness, and mediocrity, and untrimmed pubic hair, and drinking proclivities, and nastiness, and thorny opinions, and the unabashed expellant of flatulence and burps, and relative unkindness towards the ones we love, once we start taking the ones we love for granted, because love is a hard furnace to keep stoked; because accelerant is a rare and finite commodity. He tries not to be grim, though it's hard. Allowing himself one last moment of bleakness, the grim man muses: we all regress back towards humanity's gruesome mean in the end.

The wife started wearing bulk-bought underwear three years ago and she stopped going down on the unfulfilled man a year before that. The sad man was not unwilling to admit that he was not without faults. He knows marriage is a two-way road. But theirs wasn't a victim of gridlock but neglect. Theirs was a ghost town's least popular street. Though even that was more poetics than the plain and uncreative man had contributed to the relationship over the past decade.

But sex can't be unimportant! He thinks. Evolution declared, loudly, that sex was important. So our urges must, by extension, have some credence. What makes our gonads tick must level out somewhere on the biological scale of **Requirement & Significance**, if there is such a thing, registering somewhere just below autonomous breathing and smooth heart function. If something primal didn't tell us to fuck, well goddammit, where would we be then?

The elder is now six years old. He scampers back into the kitchen, frenzied for reasons unknown to even him. He's wearing only underwear and a t-shirt, a miniaturization of the old, tired man that he comes rushing at and clings on to. The man looks down. What is this thing? I made this thing? The boy opens the refrigerator and clutches onto a gallon of apple juice the way a grown man, a mountain-climber, might clutch the face of a boulder. The boy pulls with all his worldly might. Look at this cute bastard, the physically strong yet emotionally feeble man thinks, he can't even lift a gallon of apple juice! What happens next he knew would happen and yet, he did nothing.

Why?

"Get the mop," the defeated man says.

The wife is busy re-washing clean dishes. Monogamy appeared a bore but affairs seemed a hassle, appeared to be the present impasse. Their shared and secret marital truth. To call it a carnal yearning would uncork the blasé fucking heart of it: the ennui is reaching critical mass. Truth is, new genital transactions need be made, let feelings fall by the wayside.

    The children had asked for sandwiches but they now want cookies instead. How like the mother's, their caprice. They aren't worried about the fissile element in transaction, or the salesmanship that's sometime required in securing what you desire. They have no concern for the delicate nature of bonds. They don't understand that cookies, in all their refined-sugar glory are no substitute for the nutrient-enriched and fortifying power of the sandwich. God bless them. The economics of pleasure are still outside their grasp. He wants to tell them. But he cannot tell them. What you think you want isn't what you want.

    And so, at some point, he'd set off on search for the secret ingredient necessary to re-ignite their sex life. The magic powder that could spark their particularly moribund flame. It was quixotic, yeah, and only peripherally romantic, because deep-down he knew that there was no such phlebotnum. As evidenced by the long, loveless tracts of acrimonious marriages that littered their extended social landscape.

    No, he knew, it would take more than erotic things. The piss, the spit, and the shit. The interesting costumes. The coruscating gleam of leather on wet leather. The strangulating bit. He'd endeavored to learn the French words that meant mouth and digit and cock but when invoked, in coitus, sounded like something more. But even they those didn't say enough. He just couldn't build it big enough. He couldn't sink the anchorage necessary, and so fuck as he might, he couldn't complete the bridge.

    That gap would remain.

Well, last year, he thought he'd do a nice thing: take the wife and kids up to rural New Hampshire. Watch the leaves change.

Though the trip had actually come down to a vote. The alternative was some sunny Caribbean enclosure whose high, gated walls blocked off all sorts of sociopolitical strife and some real gruesome ruins-and-rubble type poverty. The Mai Tais inside, though, were free and all-you-can-drink, and there was a pool just for adults. Problem was, the four-year-old was just the older one's proxy, and so the voting bloc had a tendency to swing, generally, only one way. And so when the wife had something on her mind, she needed only convince the one. On Election Day, their partisanship was on display, and a little transparent in the man's opinion; a little gauche. The trial of New Fucking Hampshire v. Tropical Paradise saw the non-paternal family tribunal standing against their breadwinner en banc. He, and his dreams of cerulean beachscapes, and pink sand, and unlimited booze, were summarily shot down.

"I don't have to explain myself to a fucking eight-year old," the conquered man had said, dashing off towards the garage for a not-so-secret beer.

But in the end, he'd done the nice thing anyway. They all went antiquing and he overpaid about 400% for some sort of sang de bouef vase, that easily hoodwinked man. They got slow-churned ice cream from an old timey store made out of brick. Everything seemed fine. But then the wife and kids, forming a coalition even in allergy, all got sick off the dairy. So then there was the three of them, throwing up in a line under the sycamores and their gravebound foliage like it was rustic Saint Patrick's Day.

Back at home though, ah, back at home things were still in his hands.

Literally.

His cock is a thing of beauty, he postulates, even if it's only the one person who thinks so. And so when he gobbets the conditioner onto his inside knuckle-trench, then presses the wet mass against the weighty rod, and then when he feels the white conditioner slick over the fat length of it, spreading into pearlescence and then eventually into nothing, he knows, deep down he knows, that he's doing something expertly. He's summited a routine. Gained expert status. No one can jerk him off better than he can. Burning hot shower water on the neck and shoulders. The palsied crux of digits the maestro of this lewd fiddle.

But when he knew the shadow was watching, everything changed. Then, he felt less terrible. His cum wasn't his own disgusting burden, it was this man's tittered delight. Passing the cumstained buck, he knew. When the sad and stunted man was eleven he'd reached orgasm for the first time, by curious accident. He thought that first climax was a paralytic event. Thought he'd struck a wrong nerve. Oh boy. But how right was he on paralytic? At that weird, sexual fracture-point a lot of other things he had previously loved and cherished had frozen in orbit, had stopped moving, stopped mattering. And now, proof: a cord of white cum beat down by hot water. He hated making the plain comparisons, but, how much better is this than any parent teacher conference, any shrill orchestra recital? Jesus Christ. The comparison itself made it spicier. Even the holding it up against the pattern of familial boredom was a sexual trill.

Oh, if only it were so simple as lust. But it just wasn't. It wasn't about the feeling horny, and the hardened staff, or the loosing of bodily fluids. It was more than just the pathetic petit morte. Oh God, the embarrassed man thought, why this craven human requirement to be loved and admired, this incessant need for self-verification? Why do we feel this need for self-assertion of masculinity or worthiness or both? Why were we made like this, with our mirrors pointed outwards? He tried not think about it. All he knew was that what was happening, though wrong, made him feel something at a point in his life when any one thing would do. But how long could they walk this torrid plank?

Because there were times when he felt nothing.

He can remember when her mother died. What a weekend! He didn't harbor any secret animus for the lady- nothing so cliché as that. But for whatever reason, he spent that entire weekend stifling a cruel and persistent laughter. And the harder he had tried to suppress it, the stronger its desire to surface and ruin him grew. So he had to remain vigilant, like someone trying to hard boil an old egg, repeatedly poking laughter down beneath the waterline with a fork.

So, like his brethren: the unrepentant juvenile gone sent off to the principal, forced to efface only guilt and smother the inner part that wants so badly to relish in the treasured limelight of being bad lest incur more judicial wrath, the sad and dishonest man was forced to feign misery, invoking all types of macabre scenes like some sort of Stanislavskian, as he greeted and kissed wave after wave of the earnestly miserable.

Any minute now, he thought for the duration of that fraught weekend, he would be found out. Rooted out, accosted, and dragged away like a mobster by police. Paranoiac, he'd already well accepted this fait accompli. He'd envisaged his crimson curtains coming up. But they never did. The backlash never came.

And the piece de resistance of the whole charade came that night, when the wife, good and drunk and in her childhood bed, sought to grieve the way some people do. Sex is a natural analgesic, sure, but frankly, the principled man wasn't in the mood. Simulating feeling all day had left him emotionally exhausted plus there was this lingering image of the mother's formaldehyde face etched into his transitory memory that he couldn't shake, which was noisily combatting any chances of erection.

So, that night, he solidified his position as the western world's premier compassionate. His own grief too heavy an interfering agent to even make love to his adoréd wife. A fact that, stripped of context, made him seem a great sympathetic, a man with great sentimental investment, a poet. And almost no one could fucking prove otherwise. That's honestly what he thought, the next morning, eating tough bagels and clearly rotten fruit in the continental breakfast entresol at the shitty hotel, all but in the clear.

Boy, what a life! He thought. Smirking over a poppyseed.

I mean, it's all in here. All the passion, and the guilt, all the recursive cycles of shame and lust and heartbreak that make living such a colossal pain in the ass.

Don't ever tell her that the reason he remembers this occasion so vividly is because it coincided with the first time. The opening night. But, if he's being honest, the honest man will tell you: the night they'd gotten word about the dead mother, interestingly, that was the first night that it'd happened.

Yes.

And when he came that night, he felt it.

It seems it's the inevitable time to get down to logistics. The two houses, alike in dignity, were cut by a slim tract of grass equitably mowed. Party lines had been decided early on, and once the sedgy longitudes were set, a tacit agreement ruled the divvied task. The unhappy though handy man knew where it was he'd mow to, and trusted his set line would be met. The homes themselves were two fairly straightforward colonials with one vital difference;

something in the plans that the architects must have missed. There was a nook- opened with windows, accessed by a spiral-staircase, in the neighboring house's northern quarter. This would serve the vantage point. By some serendipitous luck, the upstairs bathroom of the lonely man's house, though set back off the street, featured a hip-level window. This would serve as the scopophilic platter. And there was a sightline, from **Point A** to **Point B**. The architects lacked the necessary forethought to have guessed this crucial angle. Discounting focused exploration, it should never have mattered. But from this one chance angle, any inhabitant of the windowed nook could potentially see the full naked anatomy of any unwitting bather in that neighboring upstairs bathroom. It could've gone unnoticed forever. But that angle, in one glorious moment, made this whole thing come alive.

The sad and nostalgic man can remember precisely that first lucky moment. Before the shower there was the bedroom. The trapezoid of streetlights that were directly visible from his bedroom window were burning their low orange into the evening, putting quiet light onto his front lawn, his hydrangeas. The wife was prematurely asleep, narcotized on the pills she'd took to benumb the news of her mother's passing. If he's being honest, he noticed the light on in that nook right off. He didn't notice that all-important reverse projection until minutes after. By the time he was heavy into it, though, he knew the entirety of what was transpiring here. He could feel it unmistakably, the erogenous frisson. By the time he came, the sad and histrionic man was well-briefed on the truth: that he had been performing and that the shadow had been watching. There had been a transference of feeling. That so much was clear.

Even still, he knew so little then.

Now? He knows more.

The shadow gets home late on Thursdays, usually. The lonely and expectant man, ears a-prickle, can aurally pick out the car bump and crunch over the plunge in curb and then the stone-gravel driveway. Though he pretends not to hear it. The thumps of car door and front door and the clicks of lights. Then the shadow is a firefly, guiding himself throughout the house. Room by room, the light follows him. There is no light without him.

How does this end?

Not with the actual deed. Only because, guilt always outweighs the act. The real gut-punch comes not during the event itself but with the aftereffect of remorse. You know, there was a scientist called Milgram and he wondered if all Nazis were brainwashed. Wondered if some of our actions were truly outside of our control. He tried to measure the real force of following orders by asking people to touch electrified blocks. Over and over. Which they repeatedly did, if asked sternly enough. He maybe proved that we do things even when we know it'll hurt. So forget the Gestapo subordinates pointing human conveyor belts blindly in the direction of the furnace. And then whole tribes of fair-skinned Germans flourishing in the balmy foothills of the Andes. Forget the philandering male, wantonly sticking his dick in the outlet of least resistance. And the ensuing marital discord. Forget whatever the long-term implications of our behavior.

We just cannot fucking help ourselves.

So why not strike out and grab happiness where you can find it, the man thinks, even if it burns to the touch? Because the truth is, life is sort of on a dull repeat. The lonely man sees the people in his office stir and jubilate on Friday afternoons. Friday was supposed to be life's rejoinder to weeklong melancholy but for the joyless, parental man, the weekend variance wasn't so firmly felt. Case in point:

The sad man watching television on his sad, punch-drunk couch. In this day and age, there is nothing deemed quite so sad as watching television. Like everything else, our technologic advancements have become shorthand for our ethical inferiority. "The aeroplane and the radio brought us closer together. The very nature of these inventions cries out for the goodness in men, cries out for universal brotherhood, for the unity of us all." Charlie Chaplin said that, and not so long ago either. How stupid the man had been for thinking technology was a good thing. How silly were we all? We ruined the Earth trying to make everything better.

The First World was a false promise.

And, to a lesser extent, so too feels this sad sack of shit, watching some far corner of the world streamed wonderfully into his living room. A man who never quite lived up to his promise. The kids are at school. And he's just sitting on his fat ass, because calories are wonderfully, commercially available to him and survival by way of spear-to-beast is no longer an evolutionary necessity.

Shame on him.

The comforts of modern life have turned on him; they'd reneged on their happy bargain. Because with every convenience comes a tagalong complex: every sip from the filtered water bottle invokes the image of the sad, Biafran potbelly of some desiccated African child. Everything speed-delivered and FDA-approved and microwaveable is a reminder that there are those not privy to the opportuneness of these abhorred, wonderfully pre-packaged delights.

And so the cage-free, the farm-to-table, the free-range, the humanely killed. There must be some sort of transactional fuss; some sort of "green" waylay that inconveniences the better off in order for them to enjoy their food on some second level. Like, in order to vindicate their privilege, the rich levy a little organic food tax against themselves.

Or so the ponderous man ponders, with not much left to fucking ponder about, as he slugs down blocs of syndicated television and cheap pilsner in equal measure.

It seems to everyone, the man included, that this is going nowhere.

Then, so, maybe we exit here. The gray denouement. A listless man accreting fat on a sofa so well-patronized you can see track fossils of the man's posterior worked into the fabric every time he gets up for a new beer. The weird red-white-blue light make-up of the television, changing mutely on his popcorn-eating face. The tragedy in the end not that he's been found out but, counterintuitively, that he hasn't been. He was prepared for the blowback of shame and recrimination and the resultant slander. Don't you fucking understand? He was all and ready to be crucified. Every time he'd wailed guiltily away, part of the mechanical toil was a galvanizing. Like he was steel-plating himself from the cock up. So when the sad man exits the shower, into that empty hallway, through that wounding threshold, into that cold bedroom- well, what he feels is worse. Part of his subconscious self must have been politicking for the grand reveal, all along. His rational head still careful but his heart craving the in flagrante delicto. He is not afraid. He wants the counterattack. The wrath. The ignominy. And the confirmation of pain. That, at least, the sad man thought sadly, would be something.

94

HOW TO FEEL BETTER.

Put a gun inside your mouth and pull the trigger.

(Make sure the gun has bullets.)

I'm kidding.

Start Over.

How to Feel Better by Dillon Droege.

Appreciate the expressionist byproduct of your coup de grâce. It is your brain, after all. And you prided yourself on it. Well here it is, in all its erubescent glory. (Like many an ill-formed bar graph, you may've thought, if your faculty for thinking weren't the precise thing you were ruminating over, dripping down the walls, a-ha-ha.)

But, alas, the Magritte looks better in this panel of eggshell space; such is the concessional fare of cohabitational bliss.

How to feel better? Well, you could drink every day. Drink as much as you'd like! But the intercessory episodes- (oh, don't be so dramatic, she plaints, then here we go anyway, with the dramatics) they will eventually crack through the crust and mantle, they'll dust off oceanwater, and then terrorize the major cities of the psyche. They'll clobber landmarks with wanton, puerile force. Though what do their motives matter? We are all recipients of our loved ones' precise species of brutality. Why ask the battered cheek the motive of the fist?

Something sharp: a garrote, a gibbous scythe, a chainsaw like a shark's mouth: these things might make me feel better. Suicide though, sadly, is a zero-narrative. A firm grasp on the connective essence of events, or a strong cerebral lashing-together of temporal and spatial memory, these are the signifiers of a healthy mind. I've written this exact story one-thousand times before.

This is the best I've ever come up with.

(Gibbous scythe? Don't you mean crescent? No. Don't you understand? The darkness is the blade.)

The therapist is a delicate man in a shitty suit who uses the royal we. All of the therapists have been delicate men in shitty suits who condescended to the situation in some way. What would make us feel better? He asks.

I think, I could find somewhere nice. A most picturesque diving point. And off this glorious, sunspoke apex, I could hang my toes, and spread my arms and arch my back. I could strike a diver's pose, amidst the empyrean strati.

And that'd make us feel better?

No. But redistributing my guts and bones all over this place's postliminary sidewalk, that...that might just about make me feel better.

(Here's where he was supposed to laugh.)

Do it onto a busy enough intersection and odds-on at least one pedestrian will feel a tinge of guilt walking by because their first thought when seeing the mess will be how it reminds them, just a little bit, of the raspberry jelly they'd spread on their morning's toast. Such will be the splotch we make.

We'll get close to self-slaughter. Have our own personal Bay of Pigs of mortality.

We are all kidding until we aren't.

Start over.

How to Feel Better by Dillon Droege. Leave your name out of it, Droege. You're too self-conscious for that. You know it. You hate metafiction. It's too self-aware. Too pretentious. Even saying the phrase here makes you curdle with paranoiac dread.

Start over, for real.

How to Feel Better: An Earnest Stab at Redemption by a Former Human Catastrophe

100mg, Vitamin C.
2 Gallons, water
Endless mental prestidigitation.
Riboflavin.
You feel alright.

Somewhere in the bandit's roost of your brain, there are rogue axon, trying to sabotage this very list. Drunk Dillon is standing outside Sober Dillon's virginal bed, holding a wharncliffe and wearing a white mask. He is ready to commandeer this story.

Wheat grass.
A healthy understanding of the food pyramid.
A realistic approach to the tremors of daily life.
Alright is relative.
Saboteur.

This Dillon takes comfort on a calm sea of sobriety. And when the squall comes, he is ready. His hands are ready for the heat of a slithering rope. He will keep the bow up and off-center. He will take shelter under the rippling bimini. He will feel saltwater on his face. He is ready to sing the prosaisms of the program. Yield to the higher power. He is ready to live one more day.

Part of therapy is imagining a sunny day. Here is my sunny day:

I wake up; it's cool, and no one I know exists. I don't need the drink but I have one anyway. I barely even want it. It (the drink) doesn't make me feel better because I already feel good. Some margarine sun dips into a mossgreen lake and the refraction turns the whole thing supernatural. The colors on the reeds, the brightback frogs, the reflections on the subaquatic stumps, all of it. Plugged into the sunset, the whole lake scene becomes voltaic and brilliantine and impossible.

Here, I am calm for just one more day.

I don't know how to feel good. This is what separates me from the animals. Not the opposable thumb, but an inescapable tether towards an acknowledgement of the interior heartache. I am cracking on the outside of a hard tuna can of happiness, like an ape with a blunt wrench. All of the pertinent answers are inside. All of my worldly knowledge, all that prized wit is, dumbfingered, failing against the tin exterior. So I hang my head, with simian grace, flummoxed by the implacable nature of truth.

I want to feel good. But it is harder than it looks.

I breathe, methodically.

I count to ten.

I appreciate my blessings, as I am told to do.

I picture myself swinging from a gaslight.

Because I can't help it.

You can hang yourself like all your idols!

Imitation, as they say.

There is something inside of me louder than myself. A consciousness more bold. When I try to be quiet, he steps up. He is the seiche in my tranquil lake. The lake is a muter blue, an MRI of the autumn sky, and I am supine in some swift canoe, cutting a thin ribbon through the surface tension like a pastry knife over soft icing. My canoe, I know, will tip. He'll try and wrest control.

He will end this story for me.

The therapist had another idea. If we can't feel better, maybe we could at least feel more comfortable. If we couldn't feel good, necessarily, given our present circumstances, maybe we could at least try and feel content. In no uncertain terms, this was him telling me that I was to learn to love my cage. Like a dog. My assignment was to think about how this might be possible. For us. This is what we came up with:

Suspended In A Blue Liquid by Dillon Droege

You are suspended in a blue liquid.

Or, you have been submerged completely in some strange liquid the viscosity of which is thick enough to keep you resting perfectly in place. (Color: to be determined.) You are neither rising nor plummeting. Like you might in your aforementioned lake. The blue liquid is not harmful. But we do not *know* that the blue liquid is not harmful. So, our instinct tells us to close our eyes. Life thus far has informed us that the best practice when submerged in liquid is to close our eyes and thus prevent the liquid from getting in. Old habits prove hard to break- this is exactly what we do. This is all superficial introductory stuff, our first moments in the strange liquid, which we don't even know yet is blue. But protocol dictates we keep the eyelids locked up, and so we keep them closed, for now.

It may seem counterintuitive, but even though the natural temperature of the average human body is 98.6 degrees Fahrenheit the average human body does not feel most comfortable at this temperature. This is because the internal processes that run a human body produce heat and the human body, *in toto*, is essentially one large combinatorial machine run by an interlocking patchwork of smaller machines, and these smaller machines operate most effectively at cooler temperatures. External factors like humidity and air pressure affect the ambient temperature immediately surrounding the human machine and affects also the operating temperature level of the body. This is (roughly speaking) why humans seem to prefer temperatures cooler than 98.6 degrees. The designer of the blue liquid must have understood this because (s)he keeps the blue liquid at a temperature that feels perfectly comfortable to the subjects within so long as said subject is human and of the average taste.

You say (s)he when you talk about the designer of the blue liquid because you are not sure if the designer is a male or a female. You have no kinship with this person and know nothing about them nor their motive for placing you in the liquid in the first place. All you really know is that they must have taken special care to create a liquid that is neither dense enough to cause a crushing sensation nor thin enough to make one feel as if they were sinking. The blue liquid holds you hanging right in place, like a hammock or a worked-in chair. And the temperature is such that you begin to forget about the idea of temperature altogether. You feel neither hot nor cold in the blue liquid. Neutrality, or rather, the pervasive feeling of neutrality, is a trademark aspect of the blue liquid, you'll come to realize.

So much so, in fact, that you lose mindfulness of where your body ends and the blue liquid begins. Because your eyes are still jammed instinctively shut, the physical limns of your corporal being begin to blur. Where once you felt individual fingers, you now have a vague feeling of something warmer and larger. Like an arm fit snug into a catcher's mitt. The contours of your face experience what can only be described as a sensation of filling-in. The blue liquid works like a planer of sorts. Like water slowly filling the uneven bottom of a lake, topographical features become less and less salient and then, eventually, there is only the placid water's surface. The overall feeling is a feeling of everything becoming indistinct. Whereas you used to know confidently how far your feet and your toes stretched down, you are now a little unsure, and you begin to feel as if maybe you continue down indefinitely, like the taproot of an old tree. You are no longer aware of whether you are skinny or fat because as you ride the mental elevator through the layers of your body, as you pass from your skeleton, through your musculature, your connective tissue and subcutaneous fat, the layers of your skin, you move into the blue liquid without identifying perfectly the dividing line. Like driving over state lines when there is no roadside sign. There is an imprecision of detection-memory: you are not sure where your body ends and the blue liquid begins. This- this is a desired effect of the blue liquid.

There was a time when you contemplated thrashing around wildly but you resisted the impulse, and eventually the idea abandoned you. No longer necessary because reaching out for objects is no longer necessary, your proprioceptive abilities begin to wane, and then, after an undefined period of time, are extinct. You no longer must navigate your frame through the obstacles of the world. The imperative behind proprioception has been removed. It feels a little trivial to say that you feel at one with the blue liquid but, frankly, there is no other way to put it.

You begin to feel at one with the blue liquid.

This whole time, as you've been acclimating yourself to the blue liquid, you forgot to think about breathing and, to a lesser extent, you forgot to think about eating and drinking water. This is because the blue liquid, via percutaneous absorption, has the ability to both nourish and aerate a human body. This is also by design. Feeding tubes and respirators seemed invasive. So the designer of the blue liquid, (s)he figured a way to circumvent their necessity. And so now, in the blue liquid, all autonomous and semi-autonomous systems and also the other, more democratically elected bodily functions are performed (streamlined and in-the-background, naturally) by the blue liquid itself. Because the amount of oxygen delivered to the lungs is monitored closely and calculated precisely, the pace with which the human breathes hits a mark somewhere between Biot and Kussmaul and becomes so comfortable that one hardly notices that they're breathing at all. Which is the point. The human, in this case, is you. Likewise, you never feel hungry and you never feel full. From an appetite standpoint, you don't feel very much at all.

So trusting do you become with the blue liquid you will eventually hazard opening your eyes. Having never let you down in the past, you felt it was a decision you had to make, in deference to the warm and maternal nature of the blue liquid. No surprise here, that what you see when you open your eyes is blue. To be perfectly honest, it is only the nominal blue of the blue liquid that is immediately apparent; there's nothing immediately telling of its liquidity. In fact, when you postured earlier that you were in a tank of blue liquid, it was pure speculation. There is no concrete evidence of a tank at all. And there is nothing visible that would suggest your having definitely been suspended in a liquid, and not say, a slick semi-solid, save a warm sensation that you can vaguely associate with the liquids you've known in years past. But the days of moving between the planar worlds of solid footfalls and semipermeable liquid splashdowns and aerial acrobatics through gasses seem distant in your proverbial rearview mirror, and as they peel back over the horizons of memory, their adjoining sensations lose familiarity as well. In fact, it's hard to ascribe many of the feelings that you once had in the pre-suspension world to life in the blue tank.

Now, it is only ever blue. And what of the blue? It is a dead blue. A mute and unwavering blue that neither deepens as it extends into visible space nor lightens in any peripheral way. It is not the spectrum blue of a summer sky nor the Keppel blue-green of storms at sea or the melt pewter color of those coldweather rivers that kerf through white ice and permafrost mountain foothills. It is only hard and flat and blue; unchanging in its determinate blueness. Soon, it becomes hard for you to imagine colors that are not blue. You begin to wonder if a new spectrum might promulgate itself out of this new panoptic state of blue, if hues or shades or sub-blues might begin making themselves apparent. But they do not. There is no variation in blue. You pick at your new dead spectrum with your brain, like someone trying to find the usable end of scotch tape, but success eludes you; your spectrum is a Mobius strip of a singular blue, repeating in on its blue self endlessly.

And here is where things get interesting. Because with very little else to focus on, you too begin to turn inwards. You spend your days with the memories and fantasies which reside inside your brain. You spend your days also, of course, with the blue liquid. At first, the blue liquid was a new and exciting development taking place at the tail end of the very specific trajectory your life had, up to that point, taken. In the first few days, the blue liquid represented a small, albeit prominent, portion of your thoughts and competed meekly with the vast and encyclopedic compendium of your memory. Your friends, your family, your religion, your first kitten- a skewbald little Manx named Balloon. The notion of a tank and the blue liquid it contained, wherein you resided, paled in comparison to your memories in omnibus. The blue liquid was a grain of mica at the foot of an Everest of memory. By day 50, the blue liquid was a small daisy in Everest's shadow. By day 500, the blue liquid was a man of about your size. By day 5,000 the blue liquid was roughly the size of a tank of blue liquid large enough so that a person held inside might not be able to see the walls. And because fantasy is rooted in memory and memory is rooted in your rich loam of experience, the percentage of what you now think is beginning to swell with memories and fantasies of blue liquid. All day you see only blue liquid. You see nothing else. You feel nothing else. You no longer hear or taste or smell. Blue liquid seeks the plurality in your brain.

Eventually, it will have its majority. And then it will have you completely.

Stop me here if this is all beginning to sound like a horror story. Because there is a silver lining. Eventually, you will feel better. Eventually, you will forget about what it feels like to be self-conscious about your receding hairline. You will forget what it feels like to be jilted and will, indeed, forget what the word heartsick means at all. Eventually, every complex thought you ever had will be stripped down and broken apart and its rudimentary pieces will flicker in binarity; a crude little solipsist-mechanism comprised only of the blue liquid and a nagging little notion that there is a thing called *you*. You will no longer feel the anxious burden of potential nor the terror of failure. Briefly, before these conjoined twins of a philosophy leave you forever, you will laugh about how you once let them dominate your life. Or you would, if laughing were possible in the blue liquid. Once you forget the images of the grim reaper and gravestones and satin-lined caskets and St. Jude candles you will forget that they once symbolized a thing called death.

And so you can no longer fear death.

And then everything will become perfectly simple for you. You will realize that all there is in your entire life is the blue liquid. And with nothing left to consider, you will feel a newfound command on your outlook. You will think, hey, since acceptance and fear are perspectival, and nebulous really, inasmuch that any philosophy is only ever that, just *a* philosophy, you will begin to wonder what is stopping you from choosing acceptance over fear? They are both operations. And insular ones. And so you can employ whichever suits you best.

With nothing left to do, you could *choose* to love your cage.

I mean, that. Or you could pour yourself a drink.

Except the drink on the table is the red button. Oh, and the other Dillon knows it. Still he's begging you to push it.

He knows how to make you feel better.

But he will make you hurt for it.

In our salad days, we lacked the required sample size to realize the profound agony hiding in the cyclical data.

Everything back then was a lark!

There was a time, a time when we never thought about life solely in terms of drunk and sober. And then when we did wise up, we sort of unsurfaced a possible correlation between putting the cork back into the bottle and feeling a little bit better, but what we didn't realize, was that when we would feel great, we'd only feel it momentarily. And then we'd topple headfirst from "the" wagon's brief porch into the wet dirt that we'd just laid such careful tracks over. And that there in the thin dirty water we'd feel lower than human but also secretly seraphic. Only to eventually pull on bootstraps and dry out again. Except this time, once long dry, we get blindsided by the dagger of dry ennui. Which'd cut a slow leak into a vein filled with sand. And we'd watch it sift out, powerlessly, this sand representing, in some broader figurative way, maybe our capacity for the desiccate. And we didn't know that when the sand ran out, we'd go slapping back, like some happy toddler, through the wildhydra sprinkler of non-sobriety. Wherein we'd find drenched solace, but then horror. There we find the aforementioned agony, but still we are unable to recognize the way it camouflages itself so as to not *appear* cyclic. So we'll go cold turkey. We'll let the Gobi sun of a new sobriety parch our blood again; parch it of what it requires either most or not at all. What we do know is that, in time, we will be back. We'll allow ourselves just one. We'll winnow it down to just one, just this once, until the vermiform abyss of our addiction, some self-geminating thing, starts doubling itself out so far on both ends that emerging from its blotto birthing canal means slipping right irreparably back into its teetotaler mouth, without even a moment of daylight in between. And so eventually the whole process, the relapse and refutation, the cave-in and the reprisal, it all begins to feel like a trap. Only eventually will we learn that we are trapped in a funhouse; a funhouse whose funhouse mirrors each show us something that we do not like, each mirror marbled with some grotesque anamorphic variant of ourselves.

Bartender says, "what're we having?"

It is a nice place. We order a fancy cocktail. We say,

"A Blood on Sand."

Other Dillon has tipped a domino.

These days, he'll make it seem like a minor extraction. (He permits you one fond memory of a distant time. A sophomoric romp, a few satellite beers, outside this Earth of compulsion; her summer feelings were hurt, but how? We have not yet ordinated the Newtonian Laws of our addiction's gravity. We don't yet know how they can bend and pull and break things.)

Have a beer, he says. Momentary bliss in exchange for future woe. Psychotic arbitrage, he deals Mephistophelian in. Only you can see into the future of your hangover, to see the scattered wake of it, and the undulating aftereffects of "just one."

This is his grim bargain,

The temporary sublime.

He is a creature of the now.

And starting over is not a thing.

Think of the lagoon your blood might make. Loosing a major artery in some candlelit bathroom. A created landscape of **O+**. A whole world imagined by your cut wrist, spooling outwards over the tile. There was Pangea inside of you. Some cartographer's continental wet dream. Something beautiful if viewed from above.

No.

Don't think of that.

Think of the program. But try to stop yourself before you think about its flimsy, synthetic economy.

They made you trade alcohol for cigarettes, cigarettes for lollipops. And so cirrhosis passes the upside-down torch to emphysema, and hypoglycemia caught the thing running. Death is no reaper; he is an assembly line. His little robot hands slowly manufacturing your demise. Putting your end together piecemeal. We're all just trading one form of death for another, is the sad truth. Passing the mortal buck. And on, and on.

So we fantasize about death.

Death as a form of avant-garde closet drama- something we think about, endlessly and repeatedly, but to ourselves, never ever spoken of aloud, or presented for the stage.

Death, as if it's the inverse of life. Like they're somehow just as long. When really life is the iceberg's tip, or actually, really, it's the apical cube of ice atop the berg, and even that cube's northernmost H_2O molecule, and the Earth itself, below, is death.

Death, the morose deregistration process. Filed into winding lines. Handed the appropriate paperwork. Catechized at the gate by an inscrutable St. Peter. And then all the sentences are the same. And so the gavel hits the block like waves to a beach.

Death: per capita, the best performer in the yearly GDP. Death: buy low, sell high. Except you know what they say about the death rate around here?

One per person.

So How To Feel Better? Let me sleep on it. Visions of zyklonic sugarplums tap-dancing unenthusiastically in my head.

A better title might be:

What it Feels Like to Die: An Aborted Treatise by Dillon R. Droege.

Subtopics include:

- Don't sweat the small stuff
- Realize that sweat is hugely necessary for thermoregulation
- Become a slave to your eccrine glands
- Actualize the necessary paeans
- Perform them nightly in front of hostile crowds
- Sweat all requisite stuff, moving forward

Some Roman numeral might say, submit dutifully to your job, capitulate to your sorry state of affairs. It seems like a simple binary but so much exists outside of your own compromises. This, at least, I've learned.

A cog is not unhappy. A cog is a cog. A cog rotates as told. A cog does not second guess and a cog would not expend this much thought explaining the nature of a cog.

If I could start over, I would. I would find my child self. I would warn him, but mildly. You are not as smart as you think you are, I'd say. Stay afraid of pretty girls. Stay that happy boy. Never learn a thing. All knowledge is arrows, I'd say, teetering over a scotch. Anything that makes you sharp is sharp itself. Reality'll pierce you. Take more time appreciating all the people you know will die. Take less pictures. Try and not drink, I would throw in.

Even here I don't believe in it.

If this feels like just an apologia, well, that's because it is. It is a phantom 12th step.

You have us dead to rights.

And there I am, back in that apartment, suffocating on subtext. Sitting glumly under a string of lights that are glowing their dusky little bokeh goldenrod, suffusing the room with amber light. I've got a bottle of beer and its green glass is glowing a little too.

She is also drinking. She looks handsome and radiant even with her fangs out. I forgot to warn former me about her, I think, but even if I'd known then, it'd have been too late. How do I feel better? Well, I obviously don't know. In the years that followed I'd reflect back on this moment often. I could've given this man advice. Which rooms to avoid, what clever things to say. Listen to this future favorite song.

But who is ever listening?

ABOUT THE AUTHOR

Dillon Droege is a 30-year old graduate of Fordham University. He currently resides in Woodside, Queens.

Made in the USA
Charleston, SC
06 March 2016